Praise for The Book of I

"In this lyrical and assured debut novel, Jorge Armenteros navigates us through the labyrinthian struggles of the mind of a schizophrenic painter wading through the edges of reality and fantasy... This is a haunting debut by a bold new talent."

–Laurie Foos author of *Ex Utero* and *Before Elvis There Was Nothing*

"In this powerful novel...fierce, fresh language buoys us through the many-textured darkness, shoots the whole through with crucial light."

– Laird Hunt, author of *Neverhome* and *Kind One*, the 2013 PEN/Faulkner Award finalist and winner of the Anisfield-Wolf Book Award

"Stark, poetic and haunted novel."

– Susanne Paola Antonetta, author of *A Mind Apart: Travels in a Neurodiverse World*

"A finely crafted and clearheaded book, at once sympathetic and unwilling to give any alibis, and well worth the read."

– Brian Evenson, author of *Immobility, Last Days,* and *The Open Curtain*

"His training and experience as a psychiatrist gives Jorge Armenteros a special perspective on the mysteries of the human mind, and his character Teaston reminds us that somewhere between reality and delusion lies the unconquerable world of uncertainty. A terrific achievement for a first novel."

– John Kane, MD, Vice President for Behavioral Health Services of the North Shore - Long Island Jewish Health System, and Chairman of Psychiatry at The Zucker Hillside Hospital

The Book of I

a novel

Jorge Armenteros

with art by Liselott Johnsson
and music by Sarah Wallin Huff

Jaded Ibis Press
sustainable literature by digital means™
an imprint of Jaded Ibis Productions

"What good is a writer if he can't destroy literature?"

—"Oliveira" in the novel *Hopscotch* by Julio Cortázar

TABLE OF CONTENTS

III

I am water
    People are finding me
        I think I am
            She fills me
                This is you
                    Other faces call me
                    I'm now
                        Your mind is elsewhere
                        Drunken sailor
                          Painted over him

What is a person?
    By the sea
        There is only whiteness
            That's all Phillipy can take
            He can smell the lie
                Most of me
                    There, there
                      Seems white to me
                      Don't say it
                        The sea of her skin

Things he cannot see
    I am...
        My mind with me
            Into the sea I swim
                Why your presence?
                Wait for my arrival
                    A spineless creature that needs to die
                    I wish I could laugh
                      The white foam dances

IIII

The children I never had
    Tell me, Teaston
        Even if you do not listen
            Teaston, Teaston, Teaston
            Nothing
                Marcel, don't…
                    The waves are impatient
                      Swim, Teaston, swim
                    My ruby strokes
                        Touch my body now
                        I touch her

She thought I was crazy
    Marcel looking at me
        The combustion of my life
            I?

I

Oh, but I do

Tonight I went to the edge of the cliff. The breeze blew from below, the heaviness of the sea. Far away, distinct from the stars above, the buoy moved up and down, beckoning. I am coming for you, wait, I am coming for you, I thought it said. A moment. Another. No more. My hand, the right one, dug into the white earth of the cliff. Betraying me, my very hand, my painter's hand, nails clogged with dirt, denying me the light. I did not die tonight, but I can still die tomorrow.

Yes, another day obliterates another night. I return to my studio, walk through the foyer, and enter the tall room containing a long window open to the north. When I see the image of that man on the canvas, the body exuding a blue greenish hue, the trembling carnal hands, a featureless face, the face of everyman, I spit at it. I lift a brush, its head bathed in ochre, and with quick strokes, the eyes, the nose, and the lips die. I painted over them before. My right hand lays down the paint while dirt falls off my nails adding texture to the surface.

"Teaston, leave it alone."

"Let me be, if I were to leave it alone…"

"Leave it alone, I tell you."

"Not now."

Another brush, this one dressed in dusk, smudges the last facial features. I look at him like an expecting child. I want to render him as everyman, a universal portrait, a unanimous homo, contaminated by virtues and vices, depraved and immortal. He could also be a woman. I try to paint the image, but it vanishes.

She also vanished a long time ago, my mother.

From someone's mouth, "Motherless creature."

I pause to listen. Quiet now.

The other portraits in my studio convey a story, they represent someone, maybe the idea of someone, but they are complete. I can look at them. I have never been blocked before. No, I am not blocked. I am not a painter. I am nothing.

This morning jumped at me like a jaguar, everything to the neck all at once. I resisted being anything other than a painter.

"Teaston."

"Not now, Camila."

"But, Teaston."

I had to pull away. The canvas received some lights this morning, wheat, mist, gray doubts, all the colors of yearning. I received no light. But I remained determined. This morning I prevailed.

Camila remained determined as well. And before I could touch the floor with my toe, she had appropriated my penis. The light traversing the window bounced against the wall and shined on the dead canvas, on my dead self. But all of that happened in the morning before I approached the cliff.

Camila saw me cry this morning.

"Teaston, you."

And I did not know what she meant. I did not. In spite of that, she did not let go. She held on.

The northern light wanted to go.

All of this before I went to the cliff. But later, in the middle of the day, when a stale silence grew, I attempted to paint the universal face again. So collective, this face. The moment I traced a line, with a color bright enough to conceal the deadness, a tremor attacked my hand.

Teaston, paint him.

But all I could paint was a gray line, too faint to signify.

Then came that moment. How vast the abyss. The time rushing, galloping. The afternoon burning away in anticipation of my next visit to the cliff.

"You look tired, Teaston."

"I'm not."

"What are you not?"

"Tired, you said tired."

"Oh."

The cliff lives at the edge of the sea. There, with no need to represent anything else, moist or dry, taking the wind as it comes, or wanting to roll over, like a wave of dirt boasting rocks at the crest. It falls a little into the sea every year, but it does not cease being a cliff, jagged and all. Grass grows there among the rocks, as if hiding from our view, letting the serrated edge of the rocks scare us, then the grass, soft and promising. Somehow, the more the sea gnaws at the foot of the cliff, the steeper and the more menacing the cliff becomes. One wave and then many. The waves pounding or extending their tongues soft and wavy over the rock. The sea eats slowly. But the cliff does not fall. It only bends over and points its nose to the sea. Lick me, it says, I will show you. No trees live on top of the cliff. Not because they do not dare to grow there, but because they do not crave looking like a sad spectacle of feebleness, or like worn out men; and because the trees are absent, the birds just fly by, nowhere to stand, they glide, not moving ahead, just hovering above the cliff, and watching the movements of people below. I watch the birds as much as they watch me, white, mainly white but with a few gray spots. The beaks are black, like their words. The birds do not understand. When I dig my hand in the dirt, they think I am grabbing a rock to throw at them. Self-centered birds. I am holding on to my life and they think I am thinking about them.

A mass of air revolves around the cliff. Full of salt, the air swirls and plays with the grass. The rocks are oblivious. Words get caught in the air on a regular basis. And as the air twirls and tumbles, the words get all jumbled and I hear things that make little sense. "I love to hurt you. Hurt me," I heard once. "The water, there, is just like me. Don't kill me. Raise me above the surf. I can find you under the air."

"My boy."

"My boy."

I see children climbing up the cliff, mainly during the day. I watch them play, throw stones, and tease each other. Sometimes they push each other to the edge and hold themselves back. They laugh and cry. A lot of crying arose when Lucio, the son of the major, fell down and never played soccer again. That was a little death. Grownups take pictures, or clasp each other's hands, depending on the time of day. Other times they make love.

For me, the cliff represents the edge. Life has to begin and end somewhere. And the cliff impersonates a threshold like any other, irregular. I never considered jumping until last year. Nothing special then, just life, the thought of death. Camila says I should not think too much about that. Oh, but I do.

The water beneath jumping, swallowing her complete

Camila spits my semen out of her mouth and proposes we spend the day doing something creative. I cringe. How could I leave his unfinished face, that vast field of nothingness? If I came face to face with the canvas this morning, I would paint him elongated and greenish, like the "Count of Orgaz" or "The Repentant Peter." I do not want that; I prefer to paint him as he is. And that creates the problem. He can be sorrow, he can be a sigh in the afternoon, the motherfucker can be a murderer, but at the same time, he can be an angel, a figure never known to me, sadness perhaps, or he could be the lost memory of someone I wanted to forget. I will not paint his face today. He can wait until my right hand grows numb. He can wait until Camila pulls me into the studio. But then, I would love to come again, I would not be interested in painting him.

My head comes to rest on Camila's breasts. Secure. Unabandoned for the moment, I dream of growing roots.

From my mother's mouth, "Crazy bastard."

"No, I'm not."

From her mouth again, "Crazy bastard."

No peace, no rest for my erratic mind. I dress quickly and leave the studio through the south door. The light assaults me. Bounteous, semi-bright, tinged with a dry mist, torrential. I swallow as much of its force as I can. And I descend to the old fishing port of Cassis where I sit at my table. Maybe I have no personal table per se, but my spot, my viewpoint, the precise angle from which I can see other people's lives, and the sea. A quiet moment, brief.

"Teaston."

"No."

"Teaston, here."

"I'm not looking."

Her Majesty, "The Queen of Whiteness," sits next to me. She knows. She knows I will resist. But she does not care. Her Majesty, with her elongated eyes.

"Here, have the rest of my pastis."

"Too early for a drink."

"Since when?"

"I need to paint today."

"I can imagine, all day up there... You need something else."

"Camila is here, you know."

"I know."

I look away from her. The sea reflects light as it licks the stones at the shore. Light, life, reflected light, reflected life. I need life straight. No time for anything less. Her Majesty breathes death, or muted life. But there are times when she fills me, deep, deeply.

"How about a cigarette?"

"No."

"What, is it too early to smoke?"

"No."

"So then?"

"No, I told you."

"Teaston."

"I said no."

In a different time I said "Yes." Not today. I am not ready for "Yes." Not yet, maybe later, or maybe never. The late morning asks for me. And I know it because the shadow of my hand falls hard, sharply, on the sidewalk. At no other time of day my hand leaves such a clear, firm, imprint on the sidewalk. I am nobody, even to the sidewalk.

"Teaston."

"What now?"

"Kiss me here."

"No."

"What is it with you?"

"I'm going back up."

I walk. I feel like walking. He will be up there, without a face. The same gray field of color, anyone's face, gray, or Greco green, or nothing. I can trace a line to show him better. But that will not represent him, a lie, or maybe my own incompetence. He may be laughing inside, away from the surface.

The sea grows in front of me. The meaning of climbing, to let the sea grow slowly, filling the entire horizon, the town shrinking. There is only I, and Camila, and Her Majesty sometimes, but not now. And the blank face of everyman too. Now, I only find me.

Before I go back into the studio, I glance at the cliff. The silhouettes of three people catch my attention. Tourists, I think. A woman and two men gesture at each other. The shorter of the men seems to be posing for a picture. I hear their voices, Italian, no, English, I cannot tell. Then the woman gets closer to the edge and poses too. Now they laugh. The woman's laugh pierces the air. I watch as they frolic on the edge, all joy it seems. But then, both men start descending, leaving the woman by herself at the edge of the cliff. After a while, I see the men's profiles disappear in the shadow of the ravine, down by the road. I consider walking toward them.

The woman sits at the edge of the cliff looking out to the sea. She seems

far; I cannot see the lines of her face. She could be crying, or smiling, or dreaming. The salty wind will dry her tears if she is crying, it will make her smile more ample, but if she is dreaming, the wind will blow those dreams away. Nothing left then. That is the danger.

I decide to approach her. Carefully stepping over loose rocks, patches of grass, and the fear of last night, I walk toward the cliff. As I get near, I see how she tries to keep her hair off her face. The wind insists. She sees me walking towards her and raises her right hand as if to wave, but she stops and turns her face to the sea. I come closer but she keeps gazing at the sea. I walk around her. She remains silent, ignoring me. Now I can touch her, or talk to her softly, or just stand there quietly. She seems to breathe with audacity. She lets the air move into her lungs, resting for a second, and then lets it out through her open mouth, as if smoking life. Her chest heaves, lifting a silver Bedouin necklace studded with beautiful old Mediterranean coral beads, black wooden prayer beads, and little silver crosses. She can be thinking of the afternoon, the white caps dotting the sea, or about me looking at her, I don't know. Maybe she thinks about loneliness, or death. Something could be waiting for her, unfinished, like my painting. There could be a lover, or two, maybe those two men are her lovers. I cannot see her face, only her hair, so long, so black. And the wind loves to wrap it around her face.

She leaves the sight of the sea and turns around to face me. Her face. There. The symmetrical lines, rounded around her eyes, dry eyes, clear, amber. The line of her nose, soft with a slight curvature, a daughter of North Africa perhaps. Her cheeks reflect an olive light. Lips together with a minuscule pull to the right. Half a smile perhaps, a smirk. And the angle of her jaw, brave, defiant even. All composed in graceful harmony, not completely impassive, but impenetrable enough.

She doesn't say a word. I try to listen, hoping she may murmur something. I want her to talk. Instead, the wind talks loudly by means of her hair, my shirt, and her crimson skirt, all flapping under its relentless force. She looks at me, carving her face in my memory. The turn of her face, the twisting of her body, the steps towards the rocky edge, the arms swinging up, the air, the air, the rocks bloodied, the water beneath jumping, swallowing her complete.

Nothing remains

I face him and focus on his eyes, or where his eyes live. All that paint, one layer over another, but no eyes yet. No mouth either, only a thicker canvas. He hides from me, or I hide from him, or both.

From Camila's mouth, "Teaston."

"Please, I'm painting."

I start with shadows, trying to create spaces, holes where the eyes could fall in. The color green dominates again. His eyes would fall through the canvas. I spread the paint to even out the surface. So many layers of failure, so much depth of color, still faceless.

"Teaston."

"Please."

"The *Gendarme* wants to talk to you."

I leave the canvas and head for the front door of the studio where the man in blue awaits. He looks grave and has a little notebook open. I approach him as one would approach a first grade teacher after speaking out of turn.

"Tristan."

"No, not Tristan, Teaston."

"Yes, Teaston. Did you see anyone walking by the cliff yesterday?"

"I saw a face."

"What?"

"There was a woman at the cliff."

"Was she alone?"

"Two men were there, but when I approached, they had gone already."

"Did you see the woman?"

"I saw her face."

"She jumped, you know."

"Yes."

"Were you there when she jumped?"

"She jumped."

"Yes, she did, did you see her when she jumped?"

"I saw her face."

"You told me that already."

"Yes, that's what I told you."

"You're not helping me."

I wanted to jump many times. Peer over the edge and feel the space below, full of air, full of nothingness. Life wants to come to an end. I push back. I grab on to the earth. Look at my nails; burdened with dirt, from grabbing, from not wanting to fall. Why did she jump? I don't know. Why have I not jumped?

"She jumped."

"Tristan, why did she jump?"

"Teaston."

"Yes, Teaston"

"I don't know."

What is there to know? She knew something that escapes me. Maybe that forced her to look at me, to transfer that something to me.

When the *gendarme* leaves, I return to face the canvas. I make preparatory gestures with my hand. Tracing lines in the air I direct an orchestra of colors. The strident yellows, the sumptuous horns of blues, the red cymbal, the arpeggio of ochre, and the magic of white flutes. These sounds I make in the air since my hand refuses to touch the canvas. In the background, I hear a melody, like a whisper, and I hold my hands steady to listen. The melody glides, tracing lines and making spaces. I listen to the lines forming her face, the face she showed me. I lift a thin brush and immerse it in a formidable black purplish harmony, and ready to make my mark, I return to the melody still dancing in the air. My hand and the melody touch the canvas, leaving a trace, a visual witness of her absence. I only draw the contour of her eye and she arises, looking at me again, regarding me, as furtively as yesterday.

Here I am, trying to paint everyman but the image of the olive woman takes over my gesture. No, this cannot be. My hand spreads gray like smoke, covering the contour of her eye, burying the expression under oil. Nothing remains.

Whiteness awaits me, somewhere

Not all places start in whiteness. Most often, a place reflects the surrounding colors. Just considering how light bounces from objects and surfaces, not to mention the filth and dirt, no place is born naturally white. Places become white because people need them that way. And if a place seems white, we find no guarantee that it will remain white for much longer, for all forces of nature work together to erase the whiteness from any surface exposed to the vagaries of life. A virgin place could not be white. No forests, deserts, valleys, or mountains shine in whiteness. Consider slush. An exception could be made for those beaches where the sand creates the impression of whiteness, but in close observation, we discover the grays. The intensity of the light deceives our eyes.

But I spent a period of time where everything exuded whiteness. I do not feel that way now. Even when Her Majesty talks to me with that voice of hers, I do not see anything white around me. Back then, the absence of color reigned. I remember the walls, the sheets on my bed, the uniforms of men and women who ordered me around. They all shared this absence of tonality, a whiteness only broken by their black eyelashes or red lips. At nighttime, my dreams were also white, and that disturbed me the most, the lack of shadows, even in my dreams.

That was when I met Her Majesty. In the middle of this whiteness of thoughts, she stepped forward and spoke to me. She had a white voice then. She spoke with a clarity that exuded light, and I needed that light. Her Majesty said things I had never heard from a woman. I remember the radiance of her words. No, more immediate, I can hear her words now just like then. She called me "Teaston," she said I was her boy, using my name but not telling me hers. For me she is the "Queen of Whiteness," Her Majesty is. A real queen, floating above everything in her own light.

She was prudent then, beautiful, and goodness surrounded her image, an image so regal and alluring. She spoke to me constantly and her words provided light in such a confusing time. Where she came from I never knew. But she infiltrated my days and my nights. I craved her presence then, like I crave for her absence today.

The orderlies never spoke to her, nor did they acknowledge her existence. I think the orderlies did not care. But, what could be expected from people dressed in white? Her Majesty spoke to me often but the orderlies would not listen to her. At one point I tried to convince them, by force, to listen. That landed me in the seclusion room, without windows, all padded in a white vinyl to absorb blows. I did not stay long in that room but I never tried to convince them of anything again. This did not really matter much, for I felt ready for the world outside, not a white world, a world with colors.

When I left my room in that world of whiteness, I promised I would go south where the light shines most of the year. I knew I would be able to paint, having light at my disposal. And I wanted to paint the most meaningful face, the face of everyman. But since I came here, to my studio on this cliff, I cannot resist the urge to paint the face of the fallen.

Like I cannot resist wanting to know how I came to this old port.

I am here, yes.

But how did that happened?

No, not now. That is a thought for another moment.

That woman fell and I saw her face. I need to see the tonality of her eyes again, the lines that compose her face, the angle of her jaw, even her expression. That expression propels people to look for her. And maybe they will be looking for me. I have to paint her face.

I have to.

When I walked away from the total whiteness, I did not expect to hear Her Majesty calling me again. I expected her to dissolve. But she still calls me, maybe because I need her to call me, or maybe because she despises calling anyone else. She knows me better than anyone in this town. And when I feel like my world is threatened, Her Majesty calls me, not to help me, but to let me know whiteness awaits me, somewhere.

He has not seen me

With Camila beside me, I descend to the port by Rue de L'Arène to find my table occupied. Marcel looks at me, tilts his head, offers an apology with his right eye, and points to another table. I do not follow his finger; I just keep looking into that right eye. The first extraordinary thing I saw when I came to Cassis, that eye, protrudes in a shameless way, to the point that it makes me feel desecrated. Marcel almost never blinks, and the bulbous eye becomes red and irritated with the passing of the hours. I know that vileness, mistrust, and avarice lurk behind that right eye. With Marcel, those sentiments spring out of his right eye like the juice of a lemon when you squeeze it. Camila and I stand next to the bar waiting for my table to clear. Camila doesn't mind the wait; she has already asked for a beer and converses with a young man who looks at her breasts. Marcel does not offer me a drink. He knows.

I look at him and follow his eye. It goes from the scattered bills left at a table, to the little window that opens into the kitchen, to the waving hand of a customer, which he ignores, to the sky trying to guess if it will rain this afternoon, to me, apologetic without meaning it, to his watch, back to the waving hand, "*Oui, Oui,*" to the other waiter—who looks at him and spits on the floor—now focusing on the long neck of a young woman who sits at an empty table—not mine—to the bar where two drinks wait, back to the bills left at the other waiter's table—grabs them swiftly—to Camila and the young man, then to me, a smile, and on and on until he finally blinks. I need that eye to be in my painting, I want to capture its essence, its sinister capacity to scan the world finding opportunities for meaning.

Finally, Marcel manages to insult the dignified lady sitting at my table. He must have made inappropriate comments. The lady stands up, grabs her leather bag and leaves, muttering syncopated words. Marcel clears the table quickly and gestures for us to sit down. He ignores Camila but pulls my chair. He then looks at me with that eye.

From Camila's mouth, "Teaston."

"Wait, I'm thinking."

Yes, I am thinking. Of all the places I have seen and loved, and even hated, I always come back to this one. I have been many people. No. That is not for now, that is a thought for another time.

"Teaston, look."

"I'm not looking, I'm thinking, I told you."

This port has all the elements of life and death. First, it is an old port, Romans lived here, and all of them are very dead now. Imagine, the Romans, so great then, nothing now. The extinction of life, the extinction of a collective culture, art, tastes, yearnings, accumulated envy, all very much vanished. Death very well. And life next to it, breathing the air today. The sea charges against the seawall with the energy of a raging bull, so alive, hissing. Both reside here—life, my life, and death. Everyone's death. I am drawn to this port. I look at the faces of people who come, sit at a table—not my table—drink life and feel death. They do not know they feel death, but they do.

That olive woman the other day, her face so real, so part of me, knew death. I think I know death but I do not dare. She may have had a drink

right in this very port, maybe from the hands of Marcel. She looked alive to me, and then she became invisible under the sea. This port reeks of death. This old port. Maybe saltpeter smells like that, an old death.

"*Monsieur.*"

"No, Marcel, not now."

"But *Mademoiselle* Camila said…"

"No."

Again he looks at me intently when he mentions her name. Did he really mention her name? Maybe not. I know he is designing something when he does that turn of the head to show me his right eye. Marcel is an old death who is still very alive. I can imagine him dead, but I need his right eye alive.

From Camila's mouth again, "Teaston, you…"

"No, please."

Marcel, from the death side, "A young woman jumped…"

"I know, but no."

Marcel leaves a glass of Bandol on my table. I drink half at once and think of the woman who jumped. She knows death now. But did she know death when she looked at me at the cliff? Did she know death then? Her face did not show death to me, or maybe I did not see it because the wind slapped me hard.

Two *gendarmes* walk across the terrace, laughing, as if nothing had ever happened to them or to any of us. I look away from them and my eyes land again on Marcel. He thinks I am asking for another glass of Bandol, which he promptly brings to my table.

"Teaston."

"No, Marcel, not now."

Camila takes my hand and brings it to her chest. Why not lay my head there instead? I need the comfort. The young man still at the bar looks at my hand and at her breasts now covered. Camila mumbles something I cannot understand. I feel life and I feel death, mostly death. And that makes me finish the glass of Bandol. Marcel looks at me and knows. But he does not dare to bring another glass because I say: "Not now." He does not understand. I do not want to talk about a dead woman. I do not want to face death. I can follow the face of the fallen woman from yesterday and paint it on that canvas. Not really, I already tried.

People keep coming and going through the old port. For being so old and dead, it feels very alive. That attracts me to this table. Marcel knows so well that when the *gendarmes* come again looking for me to ask idiotic questions, he tells them he has not seen me.

Yes, you bastard

She smiled often. But her lips did not curve upwards; they stayed flat, drawing a thin line across her face. She closed her eyes when she smiled, my mother. I thought she had forgotten me but she would open her eyes again. I am here. You are here. Children learn from their mothers how to smile, and how to close their eyes when falling asleep. I fall asleep now. Open your eyes. She opened her eyes, so much life in them.

Everywhere she went, I went with her. First carried in some sack, then pulled by her hand, then on my own. I remember her face going to all those places but the places themselves elude me. Do not fall asleep now, think of the places. The men she visited looked happy to see her but not to see me.

Paris seemed large, wide boulevards, people, people everywhere, and their voices populating the air. Every voice had a mouth then, and a meaning. We went into apartment buildings stuffed with bedrooms the size of shoeboxes and boring living rooms. We entered gray offices populated with desks and copy machines, and we saw desolate views from conference rooms that seemed always empty. Even the parks insinuated emptiness when we strode under the shades and I had to go and play with a stick by myself. Waiting and waiting.

Her flat smile soothed me. I always smiled back when that warmth permeated my body. With my eyes closed I smiled back trying to memorize how she looked. And at some point, when I was six or seven years, I could draw her face from memory. The features, elongated, resembled her faintly, till this day. From that moment I started bringing paper and pencil for those long tours. In the cramped apartments, under dimmed lights, I drew her face, many variations of her face. The men ignored me; they wished she had gone there by herself. One afternoon, when my mother came out from a dark bedroom, all sweaty, rearranging her pretty skirt, the man looked at my drawings. I never saw that man before. And after handing my mother some money, he also gave me two Francs for one of my drawings. I was happy; he seemed to like my mother. I never saw that man again.

I needed to draw her. And those boring afternoons in unknown places allowed me to practice. I drew her eyes round, then barely closed, like the Asian people in my schoolbooks, and then I drew them long up and down. Her mouth, I drew wide with teeth in the middle, that was early on, and then I made it flat, more the way she really looked. I could not draw her body. When I tried, the shapes did not correspond and she ended looking like a stick or a frog. The dresses did not come out that well either.

I once saw her naked and tried to draw her body.

You bastard.

I closed my eyes. I knew not to look at her when naked. But I did.

Motherfucking little bastard!

I saw the bluish scars crisscrossing her back. No, I did not see that.

Open your eyes!

No. I closed my eyes. I kept them closed.

I did nothing else but draw in those afternoons, forgetting completely about my schoolwork. It went like that for a few months until the principal called my mother into school to ask if she knew I was failing. She did not know. And when the principal asked why, she said she was a single mother and had to work very hard. Now I know she worked hard. Those afternoon visits were hard work.

The first time I knew my father did not exist was when I asked my mother for his picture. I needed to draw him too. She said there was no picture of him, that he looked like everyman. I tried to draw him, but the face of everyman escaped me. To this day. Do not fall asleep. Open your eyes, he is not here.

I opened my eyes in front of a fountain at *Le Luco*. The water was dancing. My mother had not yet returned but I did not feel alone. The droplets joined each other and I wanted to join them. At the bottom of the fountain, the water seemed at peace. But out of a cherub's horn a legion of drops jumped. They fell to the bottom and rested. This is my cycle, I thought. And removing my shoes and shirt I stepped into the fountain, splashing water everywhere and then sinking to the bottom. I saw the color of my skin change from a pinkish hue to pale mustard under the stale fountain water.

Soothing.

I did not last long submerged. I was too young to know.

I went from drawing to painting, and from listening to words out of one mouth, to words out of the unknown. I was seventeen. I know because the *Lycée* was almost finished and I wanted to date as many girls as I could. My mother did not object. She said to be kind to them, that they in turn would be mothers. I knew what she meant, but I did not know what the voices meant.

And I do not remember what my mother called me. She may have called me "Teaston." Or maybe the voices called me "Teaston." When the noise intensified and I went to hide my head in her bosom, she spoke of flowers and men who wanted to harm me, of vertical death and a hand mocking me, of salt water and, hold me, hold me, the intense pressure, blood pouring out of my eyes, of her face disintegrating, melting, dripping as fat and liquid cartilage on the dirty floor. She spoke, she spoke, she turned away from me afraid that I would hurt her, even kill her, as my mocking hand swung a blade over her in persecution of the voices, or noises. Do not say a word, let me hear them, they want me dead, let me hear them. Open your eyes now, they are not here, open your eyes.

I open my eyes.

They are not here.

She never understood how my own mind sabotaged my logic. She thought I fabricated my fears—being hunted, turning into water—she could not tell the embarrassment of having my thoughts parade for all to hear. For her, the world was practical—harsh, but practical. The visits in the afternoon, her visits to the women's clinic, my school, a hope for better times. But I always turned to her, to her bosom, for no other place comforted me.

Say it.

No other place comforted me.

Bullshit! Open your eyes and say it.

No.

Yes, you will.

She thought I was crazy and she ran away from me.

Motherfucker, what are you saying? She did, she took her bosom away from me. You miserable scum, piece of shit. She left on that boat and the river never brought her back. Not back to you because you were crazy, crazy, do you hear me? I just heard things and drew faces, nothing else. You were weird and you know it, fucking crazy bastard. Do not call me bastard. I can call you Teaston, you dirty bastard, hearing voices nobody can hear and seeing people that do not exist. Teaston was never my name. No, you are a filthy creature born from the semen of everyman. She was my mother. Yes, the motherfucking mother of a lunatic, that she was. She did not have to leave. You thought she would raise a creature like you? I am not a creature. No, you are not a creature, you are a pathetic freak. She was my mother. Yes, she was, and what difference does it make?

Now, open your eyes and say it.

She thought I was crazy.

Yes, you bastard.

Camila

I never invite Camila to my studio, or the port, or anywhere else. But she exists there, watching over my conflicted existence. I do not really know where she comes from. She seems universal. An exiled princess, or a cursed enchantress, a castaway, maybe a fugitive slave. She speaks many languages, but more important, she understands mine. One day, walking up to the studio, I saw her for the first time, a strange woman walking next to me. She looked so natural, her eyes an arpeggio of blues, her skin fresh, and her floating hair. She knew where I headed without having to follow me. When we arrived at the studio, she simply opened the door for me. I hesitated; I doubted if I needed to ask her in or if I had to say goodbye right there at the door. It did not matter; she went into the studio ahead of me. She then turned around and said:

"Teaston."

"No," I said, when I really meant, "Yes."

She spoke about her need to see the ocean from high places, about the language of painting, about her love for music, and that she had seen me before but only now dared to speak to me. We met like that many times, never talking about her or where she came from. I waited every day to find her along the path, and every day she joined me on the way up to the studio, and every day we stayed longer a longer together. Sometimes, we would look over the sea for a long time, not saying a word. One day, she did not return to wherever she came from. She stayed with me. And ever since, when I am painting in the studio, she is there. When I am away she walks. She always follows me to the port, to my table. But not to the cliff, she does not follow me there. She fears the cliff. Maybe she fell off a cliff once, or maybe she knows she could not help me if I wanted to jump. I can always tell when she hovers around because the air feels warmer. And then she touches me, and ever since.

When I paint I need to be alone, Camila knows but still comes around. She looks at the way I lift my brush, my gesture, the way I layer one coat of paint over another. I know she watches me but I pretend she is not there. In silence, she looks at me painting and destroying what I just painted. She never makes a comment. Only when she walks farther away, distant enough not to see the canvas, would she call me.

"Teaston."

Camila says she does not need to know her future. I believe her. I believe she arrived here without knowing why. One day I may transcend being a painter, she may join with me, or not.

I try not to call her. But there are moments when I need to lay my head on her bosom. She can sense my yearning and then calls me softly.

"Teaston."

"No."

But she knows I mean, "Yes."

Camila.

A dominant shadow

I forget Her Majesty this very moment. I close my eyes and pretend I never met her. "Teaston," she would say. But I don't care. I forget her right now. Look, her name does not register anymore, no reaction when repeated: "Her Majesty, The Queen of Whiteness."

Nothing.

My fingers do not tremble, my breath flows smoothly, my heart rate runs steady. I say "Her Majesty" again and my mind registers nothing.

My thoughts rest in order. But when I see glints of whiteness, all the demons come out. And from a white shadow I see her face emerging. I then say "Her Majesty" out loud to dispel the image. It does not work very well. Oblivion, I have tried it. Her image deepens in the whiteness as a dominant shadow.

Grabbing the air

The breeze feels mild this time of the year, kinder than the dreaded Mistral. I let go of the line and my little sailboat starts floating away from the mooring. I pull the main and go. Me, alone now, without them, only the wind accompanies me, aiming the boat toward the foot of the cliff. The sea swallows my path, I leave no trace, a ripple. I doubt if I need to see the woman who killed herself come afloat. I think at first I want to see her, but then I decide I do not. Her face would look gray and bloated, not the face I saw at the cliff. My face saw her face last. Why did she choose my face to carry with her? She saw something. I turn into the wind and let go of the jib and main, all flapping now. When the boat calms down I lean over the starboard gunwale and try to find my reflection on the surface of the water. Too choppy. From the immense blue I look up to the cliff trying to identify the spot where she last saw me, where I last saw her. Her fall was jagged; she hit the rocks before reaching the water. I would not like it that way. I imagine for myself a clean fall, nothing between the sea and my death. Maybe the rocks reshaped her face, those lines I cannot erase. It does not matter, I still remember them.

The waves and the wind push my boat closer to the rocks. I regain control by making one tack, then another, and I come around clearing all trouble. I will not go down this way, by accident, like a fool. I will give myself to the sea; the sea will not claim me. I only look for her face because mine was imprinted on hers, as hers is imprinted on my memory.

The illusion to see her face again brings me here. She hides from me, she does not float with her face up to the sky for me to see. The sea saw her face last, not me.

My boat feels oblivious of the people that fall to their deaths or the corpses that emerge from the deep. My boat only responds to wind and current, it shrieks and howls, it yowls and moans, when the elements beat her. But for the most part, my boat is hollow. And when she cries, tears sipping through her hull, I comfort her, plugging her open sores.

As I head back to port, my boat seems to sink below me, falling off my feet. Soon I believe I am sailing underwater, the fish swimming by my side, the algae blocking my vision, and the hulls of multiple boats bobbing on top of me. I sail underwater and my hair flows behind me in the current as I glide through a sea meadow under the Mediterranean. My hands lose their red color and everything turns a bluish green. I see a familiar world, imagined only from the angle of my table, where I sit comfortably and look over the harbor, Marcel, looking at me with his right eye, while I wonder what stories lie below the surface of the blue Mediterranean water. This world resides here, underneath. Once I recognize all the bearings, upside down, I feel safe at harbor. I throw the anchor and I see how it ascends like a kite to the surface of the water above me, grabbing the air.

I sense she exists

A stretched canvas. I have painted faces on so many of them. My right hand pours the colors and a face grows out of it, or more precisely, a person emanates from the oil. The faces I paint look pathetic, a failure in verisimilitude. My hand paints distorted faces, not elongated like the faces of El Greco, but not anatomically accurate either.

I need to watch my hand; it does things on its own.

The time I painted normal faces, before the whiteness, was a dead time for me. Normal people bought my normal portraits. What did they know? Now, I only want to paint that aspect of a person not reflected on their face, hidden from their visible self. It all comes out somewhat odd, but so be it. Camila says I should paint what I see. Not so easy. I see a lot, but much more hides from me. Like the woman who jumped from the cliff. I only saw a little of her and I bet plenty escapes me.

But here you are. What do you think you are? You motherfucking canvas.

Enough.

I fasten the canvas to the easel and place it in the middle of the studio. The northern light shines just right, not too intense, and not too feeble either. Camila sees what I do and sits at the corner of the studio, watching me, ready to comfort me with a word, the same word I yearn to reject.

I take a brush in my hand, it pulsates, it doubts, it spreads a deep burgundy in the place where a mouth should be. Then the color of sand makes a field of hair. Camila watches but says nothing. I stand in front of the canvas and let my right hand draw a few lines with a charcoal pencil. Another color, maybe pale purple. Then a reddish brown. I see how the mouth looks out of place, yes out of place, and the eyes seem displaced too. I cannot watch the face that forms in front of me.

My body shakes.

Let me be, I tell myself. I need to paint him. I take another brush and hold it on my extended arm until my hand stops shaking.

Easy, easy.

My hand wants to attack the canvas, to imprint some life into the face, but I hesitate, I have to slow down. I stand and wait for the tremor to stop. Black, black, I force black above the burgundy. There is no stopping; I just continue pouring paint, all colors, blurring any trace of reality, distorting the face of nobody.

Camila, Camila.

She looks at me knowing her comforting words would serve no purpose. And the paint drips, forming a dull smirk on nobody's face. This is not the man, this is not the woman. I open a large container of white paint and sink both of my hands into it. I grab as much white paint as my cupped hands can handle and throw it against the canvas.

The white paint runs down and starts to drip from the bottom edge of the canvas. My hands drip white paint and my mind goes white for a second. White eliminates all other colors; it purifies, it brings back everything to an original nothingness. Camila looks at me and I can see the frustration on her face. Somehow I arrived at this studio, running away from everything I knew, to come out of the whiteness. Whiteness everywhere, walls, people's dresses. I found the solitude of the studio and the light of Cassis perfect to paint one face only, not the face of nothingness, quite the opposite, the most revealing face, a face naturally distorted by its complexity, the face of everyman.

I retreat, my hands like white gloves. Camila asks me to sit next to her and I agree because I need grounding. Camila, please. She takes my right hand and brings it close to her face.

"Open your hand, Teaston."

"My hand."

She holds my open hand and presses her face against the palm. With her eyes closed, she moves my hand all over her face, my fingers spreading over her nose, her lips, painting herself white. She then takes my left hand and paints her neck, her ears. She disappears like the face in the canvas, the lines of her face vanishing into whiteness.

"Teaston, I'm Camila."

Everything so white, the shadows white, my hope of painting white, a white Camila that claims to be Camila. I kiss her, and I feel as if I am kissing nothing, the whiteness of nothingness.

"Teaston, I'm Camila."

"Press your face against mine, don't move, stay there, just there."

She does not know. She does not know about the places I have left, about the enclosed places, white over white, where nothing made sense. Here I fail at painting, and the fear of my thoughts breaking down, like trains derailing or crashing into each other, threatens me. I may jump off the cliff one day, perhaps, but at least I know I want to jump. I know it.

Camila came to me out of nowhere, not knowing that I escaped from the white nothingness. And that pleases me. I may not know all about her, but I sense she exists.

My boy

She must have a sixth sense because as soon as I turn the corner of Rue Frédéric Mistral, Her Majesty looms over me. No one can tell from what angle I will approach the old port, but somehow she can. I have tried taking different roads hoping to confuse her. But no, she always turns her canine nose toward me and smells me from far away. I don't look at her. That matters very little because she smells that I am aware of her, destroying me that way. The awareness is enough, she does not need to talk to me, or even look at me. All she needs to do is create the certainty of her presence and the rest follows.

Her Majesty was not a dreaded presence before. She became one. I do not remember exactly when this happened but one day, in the winter, I believe, she embraced me and I felt this strange chill slicing my brain in multiple segments. And from that moment I have been avoiding her. I know she hovers somewhere, around here somewhere, right this minute. But I will not turn to look for her. I hate for that sable to slice my brain again. I feel naked and cold when that happens.

She knows about Camila. She has never spoken about Camila, and perhaps she has never seen her, but she is aware of her existence. Her Majesty, how could she not know? Some times Camila joins me here at my table, in that manner of hers, all subtle and surprising, and then that sense of Her Majesty sniffing me disappears. Camila does not know about Her Majesty, why should she?

Only last week Her Majesty threatened to jump from the cliff. I refused to look at her, even if she threatened with jumping. She was playing with me because I am the one in danger of jumping, not her. Sometimes I think she knows what I am thinking, even when my brain waves could not reach her. I wish for Camila to join me here at my table and not have to deal with Her Majesty looking at me like that.

Her Majesty never went to my studio. Much better, I need peace and quiet to finish painting everyman's face. Camila feels at home in my studio. Intrusive, yes Camila is, but I prefer that to bearing the look Her Majesty lays on me. But I do not understand why Her Majesty never made it to my studio. I think she never wanted to see my painting. Or maybe she would not want to see me jump off the cliff. All pointless because I have not finished the painting, nor have I jumped, yet. It must be Camila that keeps her away.

I sit at my table and Marcel brings me a glass of Bandol, Mourvédre-dominated, totally uncompromising, firm, firmer than myself. I enjoy a first sip and let the sun warm me, relaxing my jaw. The image of the fallen woman arises unannounced. The line of her mouth and the angle of her eyes, her oliveness, the abyss behind her, the sea below, no fear.

From Her Majesty's mouth, "Teaston."

Impossible, truly impossible.

From Her Majesty's mouth, "My boy."

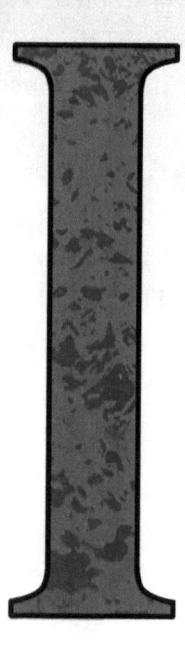

II

I hate him

Marcel knocks at the door of my studio. For a moment I think the *gendarmes* returned with more questions, but when I open the door, I encounter Marcel carrying a black leather bag, his eye pulsating, and next to him a little man that looks like his son, a child of sorts. He is taller than a child but shorter than a man. His shirt binds him tightly and his pants are too short. His chiseled features look like those of someone who has lived for a while, but his eyes, his expression, resemble those of a juvenile, a person who marvels at the world. This man/child seems frightened, and when I ask him to come into the room, he squeezes past me, making sure not to touch me. Both stay close to each other forming an aberrant mound in the middle of the studio. They do not embrace, but they stay very close to each other. The man/child averts direct eye contact while Marcel impels me with his right eye. Marcel has never come to visit me here, so I assume this to be a serious matter.

"Phillipy, look at Teaston, and say good morning."

"The morning is good."

"Look at him."

"I know he's there."

The man/child smiles at the air and ignores my extended hand. He remains close to Marcel while turning his face away from me. I retrieve my hand understanding that there will be no handshake; after all, there is no eye contact either. I offer Marcel a chair but he can barely unhinge himself from the grasp of the man/child.

"This is Teaston."

"You told me already."

"Let go, Phillipy, let go of me."

With force, Marcel gets loose and sits at the chair. I pull one of my stools and sit across from him. The man/child walks towards the entry and stands facing the closed door. He seems at ease with his back toward us.

"He wants to paint, Teaston. Maybe he can learn from you."

"But who's he?"

"My son, my son, Phillipy."

"I've never met him."

"He keeps to himself."

"Is he..?"

"Phillipy, tell Teaston that you want to paint."

"Marcel already told him."

"He has talent, believe me. Phillipy, don't you know how to paint?"

The man/child utters a grunt. He remains at the door rocking and twirling his fingers in front of his face. Marcel opens the leather bag and pulls out two bottles of *Domaine Tempier*, the finest of Bandol wines.

"He's a fine boy, Teaston."

"But what's his name?"

"I told you, his name is Phillipy."

"Is that who he is?"

"He's my son, Phillipy."

"Yes, that's what you said."

"Take these bottles, they're for you."

Marcel points his right eye in my direction. He scrutinizes my face, my soul even, and then his eye wanders all over my studio, taking measure of the walls, the northern window, and the unfinished canvas. He perspires profusely, not because of the long climb to my studio, he came by automobile, but because of something else.

"No, Marcel, I cannot..."

"I convinced the *gendarmes* that you were harmless."

"What?"

"The *gendarmes*, they ask all sorts of questions."

"Marcel, what are you saying?"

"I don't say anything, which *is* what I'm saying."

The man/child moves away from the door and walks towards Marcel. He stands next to him in anticipation. He taps on his arm as if asking permission to speak. Marcel rubs the man/child's arms back and forth. The man/child smiles, his eyes closed, his face shining.

"I can paint you."

"Do you know who I am?"

"You're, Teaston, are you not?"

"I don't really know."

"I can paint you the way I see you."

"What do you see?"

"I don't know. I haven't looked at you yet."

Marcel takes Phillipy's hand and leads him out of the studio for a moment. I hear them speaking outside but cannot discern what they say. This child, or man, or whatever, knows something about me, or maybe he does not know anything about me but possesses the ability to see beyond the surface, beyond my facade. Marcel's comments about the *gendarmes* make me uncomfortable. What do they want to know about me? Why does this man/child want to know about me? Even my name, does he know that I have been looking for my name? Maybe Marcel knows that I have gone to the edge of the cliff. Maybe he wants me to bring this creature of his to the edge of the cliff as well. No, that is ridiculous.

After a few minutes of intense discussion outside the door, Marcel returns to my studio and announces that Phillipy had to go back home, that, with my permission, he would like to come back at another time and watch while I paint. He did not explain much, like Phillipy's age, the whereabouts of his mother, or whether Phillipy is a normal person. This last point may be irrelevant to Marcel, but for me, the existence of normalcy is a primordial question. I accept Marcel's plan and stop wondering about this man/child. I do not simply forget him, how could I since he asserted my identity as Teaston, an assertion I cannot make myself. I just displace my curiosity and lay it on Marcel instead.

"Is this really your son?"

"Who else could he be?"

"I don't know, he could be a distant relative, or something like that."

"Is this your studio?"

"Yes, where are you going with this?"

"Well, then, he's my son."

"Unlike you, he doesn't want to look at people."

"Neither do you."

"Marcel, I look at people, I look at them very well."

"And they get an urge to jump from high places."

"Is this what you told the *gendarmes*?"

"I told the *gendarmes* you were a painter."

"Did you say anything about the woman who jumped?"

"How could I? I don't know anything about her."

"Did they ask about Camila?"

"Who?"

"Nothing, nothing."

I turn my back to Marcel and take a few steps away from him. Sometimes I say more than I need to say.

"What's the matter with Phillipy?"

"He's just in his own world, that's all."

"What world is that?"

"His own world."

"Why do you bring him to my world?"

"He doesn't think about this as your world, he thinks this is an extension of his own world."

"How do you know that?"

"He thinks that way, he always did."

"Can he really paint?"

"Figures, faces, everything, He's very talented."

Talented. Talented. Everyone is talented. Everyone who can finish a painting has talent, even if the painting is a pedantic effort, an exercise in vapid self-expression. What could a man or child paint if he lives in his own world and thinks the world of another is also his? I loathe this kind of creature. Marcel's son, Phillipy, whatever his name is, I am determined to detest him. He did not look at me, but he knew who I was. Just because of that, I hate him already.

I hear my name again

What is a canvas after all? A surface, a projection, a requiem? What can fabric and pigment tell anyway? I used to think that way. I still think that way. But then, why would I destroy one image after another?

To destroy, what a hard verb.

Why would I paint over what I painted before?

Never again.

Here, I select the color amber, no, not the smelly blubber from whales, but the color, honey and translucent. I layer some over the edge of the canvas, and with a medium size brush, I move it, as if a sheet of morning was dawning. Then with a stick of charcoal, a faint outline, just the outline, there. Who cares? Velazquez would have laughed, so would Goya. My hand wants to show what my mind can see. My hand wants to draw her profile, the one before the fall.

"Teaston."

"Not possible, not now, I'm painting."

I ignore the call, I ignore the time, and I ignore my doubts. I lift the other brush, the one dripping in a color I cannot describe, a reddish tone, far from blood, closer to the sun in the afternoon, a red not so red but sad and violent. The pigment smashes onto the canvas in spite of me. It forms a shadow, an outline, a promontory, intense as it is elusive. And without clear outlines, I identify a slender portion of her outline, that impassive expression that held up in the air before she fell.

"But, Teaston."

"Hell no."

They can call all they want, I am painting now.

"Teaston, Teaston."

A space opens in front of my eyes. It expands and becomes a room, a large cavern with yellow stalactites and stalagmites, up and down, down and up, dripping water, while a stream of words flows among them. I see my name going by, precious. It goes "Teaston, Teaston" and I follow its little tail trailing behind. The space inhales and exhales, and with each exhale, an old sweet and musty breath covers my face, and with each inhale, I feel a force pulling me in. A force pulling from a center away from mine.

I fall.

As I fall, I see those faces that made the journey, the ultimate journey, from the top of the cliff to the sea, deep, deep, deep.

Who could resist?

His face emerges now, the one that evades me, the one that keeps hiding under multiple layers of paint. He also jumped, but how long ago, three months or three centuries? Maybe that makes him vanish, or more appropriately, I make him vanish with my own brush and paint. I hate old things, old deaths.

And now her face, again that olive tone, fresh, a fresh death she is.

I trace a few lines with my right hand. Then I close my eyes to the northern light and let my right hand trace other lines on its own, in darkness. When I open my eyes, I discover traces that resemble a rock. I close my eyes again and allow my right hand free range. It moves in circles, diagonally, slow and fast, it punctuates, it launches an attack, it stops as if resting or doubting, then it smudges paint and more paint on the canvas. I see the sickly white color and the jagged roundness of the cliff.

I hear my name again.

One over the other

I admire the start of the day.

Nothing pinned down, agreed, or accepted. When the weather remains a mystery. When I don't know my name, I mean, when they have not bothered to call me yet. Not yet. Not at this time of the day. Moving into a day like this, clean, with no memories, only the certainty that I have arrived at this moment, makes me vibrate. What moments. I know this will not last.

"Teaston."

I knew, I knew perfectly well.

"That's not my name, that's how people call me."

"Teaston, will you?"

"No, no."

I grab my hat, the one that makes me look like a sailor, not really but almost, and dodge all eyes, calls, or hugs, and step out the door into the morning. This will be easy. I start walking to the battered '71 Citroën, a decade old now, when I look at the cliff, that hump far across the field, that white and green whale of a hump from where people like to catapult themselves out into the void.

I am not looking.

Yes, I am.

Fine, but just for a second.

That's it, no more.

I release the brakes and let the Citroën coast downhill, put it on first gear, turn the key 180 degrees clockwise, and let the clutch out. The Citroën coughs, and then roars. What a fine way to destroy a fine morning. And the cliff there, for me to see at this early hour. I open the window and let the morning chill comb my hair and dry the dawn tears from my eyes. What a fine way.

The day promises nothing. No more morning available, not this one at least. Tomorrow…well, it depends on my right hand. The number of hours between now and later expands and contracts in response to something I don't want to consider. I know the voices will kill me.

Did I say kill?

Kill, call, kill.

No, not really. The voices will call me. That I count on. I will try to advance my painting. Sure, the day promises nothing.

As I walk from that Citroën machine into the old port, I realize the morning is lost, or at least violently damaged. I walk in front of Marcel and ignore him on purpose, but his right eye burns a hole in the middle of my morning.

"Ready for a morning Bandol?"

"Don't mention time, Marcel, don't."

"This is your morning."

"I know."

Not even when he blinks I am relieved of the intense rays that emanate from that retina of his, reflecting light, intense light. I find a certain malignancy in that light, reaching me and burning my apprehensions. He tortures with that eye, he unmasks lies and threatens. Malignant, yes, malignant.

Conjure, I do, all possibilities to survive this day. I think of those faces that fell, the ones that breached the void. But the cliff offers no void. The cliff opens a passage to a real space, not a void. Plenty of phenomena exist beyond the cliff: air, beautiful views of the coast, thoughts that expand and occupy the immensity of a second, a memory of childhood, then water. Not a vapid void, but a fluid surprise. But those faces come into my mind and fight for a place on my canvas. If I hope to survive this day, I will need to allow them.

"Do you want your Bandol now?"

"No, not now, it's not time yet."

He should know. But when he sees me this early he gets confused. The whole day, that's all, not more than that left. I feel my right hand burning

to trace an eye, or a lip, or the expression of sorrow. Not my sorrow, I have none. But that man, he scares me a little when he surfaces from so many layers. Or perhaps that olive skinned ghost of the other day. Layered up and buried under oil and pigments nonetheless.

All day ahead of me, and the opportunity to sacrifice every hour, to turn the sand clock into a butterfly. With a rehearsed whip of my hand I signal to Marcel. And within minutes, a glass of Bandol lands on my table, and olives too, the good ones, black and spicy.

All day, all of it, ahead of me.

The glass of wine lasts as long as it takes me to drink it. Why would it last longer, or why would I rush to finish it? At the end, the entire day rests on its back, perhaps smoking, but clearly waiting for me. It has nowhere to go. Camila rests up there too, where else could she go?

Semi-satisfied, I head for the Citroën and hope it will deliver me to the top of the hill. The light must be pouring through my northern window now. I trace figures in the air. I will paint his face, her face, his face, her face, one over the other.

She took death

"Can you tell us more, *Monsieur* Tristan?"

"Teaston, please. Remember I told you it was Teaston?"

"Yes, yes, but my colleague here doesn't know that."

"Well, I didn't know that woman. I don't know her now, either. But maybe I know her face."

"Do you know her?"

"No, no. I saw her face, I know her face now, but I don't know her."

"Teaston?"

"Yes, Teaston. You said it correctly."

"Teaston, you saw that woman before she took her life."

"I don't know if she took her life with her."

"She took her life, she killed herself."

"She jumped; I don't know where her life went."

The *gendarmes* stare at me with derision. They ask questions, I just answer. She left her life somewhere; I know she did not take it with her because her face reflected a transparent light. She must have parted with her life before throwing her body into the sea.

"Have you seen her before?"

"I've seen her expression before."

"So you know her."

"I know her face."

"Then you know her."

"No, no, I know her expression."

"*Monsieur* Teaston."

"Yes, Teaston is correct."

"*Monsieur* Teaston, did you speak with that woman before she jumped?"

"No, but I would've wanted to speak with her."

"Why?"

"Because of her face."

"What about her face, *Monsieur* Teaston?"

"I've seen it before."

"Where *Monsieur* Teaston, where?"

"In my own mirror."

The mouth of one of the *gendarmes* bends to form a half moon under the tip of his nose. The other *gendarme* looks away, far away into the horizon. They seem bothered, disappointed maybe. They make me sign a few documents. One speaks on the phone and says they do not have a body, that they have not found it. For a while, I feel ignored or abandoned by the two *gendarmes*. But after a few minutes of uneasy silence, they escort me out of their office and into the streets of Cassis. I know I will see this pair of *gendarmes* again. I just hope they will remember to call me by my conjectural name.

The streets spread away from the old port like sunrays. They gather all the energy from the sea and spread it further up the hills. Death seems to travel in the opposite direction. It originates anywhere, up on the hills, inside houses, over promontories, within ravines, finally merging at the apex of the old port. Like a funnel, the terrain drags all negative experiences down.

I saw her face, luminous. And when she jumped her life went elsewhere, but her body, the one bloodied by the rocks, the deadly one, certainly went down into the apex of a bad death. Why did she choose that cliff? Why did she wait for her friends to leave before jumping in front of my face? Why did she look at me and yet did not smile? She knew death was available, and she took death.

Closer to myself

A thick plastic covers my mattress. I never pee on myself at night but they still cover the mattress in plastic. A white plastic, like the walls, like everything around me. I wish to pee in the corner of this blank seclusion room. No, better not. There will be consequences. Somnolence, medication induced somnolence. I will not pee in the corner, but let me out to pee like a man, in the woods.

"Let me out!"

"Fuck off, Teaston."

Just for knowing what they know. They keep me here because I know them. They feel exposed when I tell them what they think. Girlish men, a bunch of lame motherfuckers. Their faces, I should paint them, when they hear their own thoughts, revealed, blasted out in the open. No, I do not read their minds; their minds just talk out loud for me to hear.

"I need to pee."

"Drink it, Teaston."

That name again. They call me "Teaston." I never heard that name

before. But they use it constantly, as if I were someone called "Teaston."
Who cares about a name? I will get them.

"I'm Teaston, and I need to pee."

"Can you read my mind?"

"No."

"Can you tell if I will let you out?"

"I don't know."

But I do.

They open the seclusion room and escort me to the bathroom. My
bladder is about to burst, but I remember the somnolence—that taciturn
experience—and hold it until I reach the urinal. I let go, liters, and a
vaporous miasma rises. Alone, inside the bathroom, I feel liberated, all
white still, but liberated nonetheless. And when I turn around I see a
female figure watching me. Her voluptuous body wrapped in torn and
raggedy clothes, and a fetid smell of alcohol oozing from her.

"That's all mine."

"What?"

"Don't be shy now."

This woman grabs me and holds my head tightly between her legs.
The stench makes my stomach revolt. I hear her laugh. She keeps her hold
and my projectile vomit bathes the inside of her thighs.

"My beautiful boy."

"Let me go."

"Stay between my legs."

"Let me go."

"Dear, dear, boy of mine."

"I'm not your boy."

"I'm your Queen, my boy."

One of the orderlies opens the bathroom door and a torrential light
floods the space turning everything white on white. I lie on the floor with
vomit all around me. He looks at me with the expression of people who

want to hurt, to humiliate, to dehumanize.

"Look at you, Teaston."

I cannot look at myself. At least, I cannot look at myself as "Teaston," for that is not my name. I cannot look at him or look at that queen who wants to rape my mind. Who does she think she is? Her Majesty? Her Fucking, Slutty, Majesty?

The orderly escorts me to my regular bed. This extensive bed in this expansive room, better than the little cell, but hellish still, for the voices continue their assault. I get into bed and burrow my way under the musty covers. How small my world now. I breathe my own exhalations wishing to reach the outer world; I must leave this sickening whiteness and find the sea.

An entire day under the covers. I am untouchable here.

In the morning I sit at the edge of my bed and peer down the precipice. No, this is not the sea. She comes, the nurse, balancing the little silver tray with a plastic cup containing numerous pills and a paper cup filled with water. Somnolence pills, not silencing pills as they claim. I know because the voices keep getting louder. I take the plastic cup and dump all the pills into my mouth. She allows me to do it myself because I behaved well yesterday. My tongue twists and turns and pushes all the pills against the inside of my cheek. I grab the cup of water and drink it all in one big gulp, making sure the water flows past my tongue directly into my throat bypassing the pills.

"Have a good day, Teaston."

When she leaves the room, I spit out the pills and add them to my collection under the mattress. These pills are for Teaston, they are not for me. And I do not care if they find them later because I will be gone, I will be by the sea.

In the afternoon they take us outside to the courtyard for air and sun. A vestige from the consumption era when air and sun failed to cure a single soul. But my kind nurse wants me to hear other sounds, the birds perhaps, or a cricket. Around me, men and women sit on concrete benches smoking as many cigarettes as they can in the tight one-hour period. One hour. That is all the time I have.

"Teaston."

"No, not now."

"You came out of me."

"I'm not Teaston."

"Come back, come back inside."

"I'm not your son."

The men and women focus on smoking their flaccid cigarettes. I walk around the courtyard staying as close to the walls as possible.

Thirty-five minutes left.

The sun reflects its light against the walls creating an avalanche of whiteness all over us. No orderlies stand by the open southern door.

Twenty minutes left.

"My little boy."

"I'm no boy of yours."

"Just taste mama's juices."

"Close your legs."

"Right in here."

I run.

I close my eyes and I run.

I close my eyes and dash straight for the southern door.

Ten minutes only.

Outside the courtyard a vast field of unkempt grass extends for several meters. After the grass, trees stand tall holding many bird nest. I know because I can hear them. The voices chirp in high tones, so many birds. And the closer I get to the trees, the louder the chirping gets.

I run.

I enter the woods and the cacophony of sounds overwhelms my senses. Who is talking? Who wants what? I see them flying, the birds, mocking me, calling me names. "Teaston," and who knows what else they call me. I run more, I keep moving south, to the sun, to the edge of the sea.

Time is up!

I am out.

When night falls, I find myself far away from the whiteness. I walk for days, maybe centuries. People greet me and despise me. My face grows hair. Night and day follow each other, mainly in that order, but at times it feels like night follows another night. I then wrap my arms around my knees and rock back and forth on the bare ground.

Salt in the air as I walk south.

Salt in my mouth.

La route du sel serpentines in front of me taking me closer to nothingness. Maybe closer to myself.

Salvage nothing

First the empty buckets with remnants of paint, those witnesses of failed attempts, then my stool, the revolving one, tubes and tubes of emulsified pigments, that easel holder of nothing, then brushes, linseed oil, linen canvases, rags, all of this I throw away from my studio but not from my mind. Everything comes out. Camila watches as I eviscerate my space. She sits on the floor, her legs extended in front, slightly apart, her extended hands behind supporting her back, like a switch blade. She looks at me with that look. I know she prepares to say something, but she does not. I marvel at the weightlessness of my empty studio. The northern window funnels a pallid light into the space making the dust particles dance.

At the end of the empty room, a lone canvas reclines against the wall with layer upon layer of faceless faces. I can sense its weight. I walk outside and let my eyes do exactly what I promised not to do, stare at the green and gray cliff. I sense its massive weight. Between these two colossal bodies, the unfinished canvas and the cliff, my own body feels feeble—a twig.

No, no, the canvas must come out, I think, while Camila watches me grab that stretched piece of cloth and place it outside the studio, making sure the repainted surface faces the stone wall. I do not intend to punish the canvas, but I do not want the canvas to see the cliff, or the cliff to get ideas from the canvas. It needs to be this way. I am alone, and they know it.

"Teaston, you..."

"Don't say it."

Camila always calls me when I cannot answer. But then, she looks at me with tenderness, as if sensing something, something indecipherable, something I cannot put into words. Camila, only you.

I walk back into the empty studio and confront the fear of nothingness, the fear of a child ignored by his mother. Everything is outside, where am I? Inside the empty studio the face of the olive woman floats, and the air filtering through the northern window keeps it from touching the floor. I imagine the sound of her body as it crashed against the rocks, before sinking into the clarity of the sea. She had a face, and a solid body, I have none of that.

From Camila's mouth, "Teaston."

"Camila, can you hear the sound of the body?"

"I can only hear your echo, try again, sing a song."

"I'm not playing."

"Teaston, play with me, say: 'Camila, darling.'"

"I'm not playing, I told you."

"You say so many things, say: 'darling Camila.'"

"Can you hear that thrashing sound?"

She cannot hear any sound. The studio repeats my words but not the sounds from several days ago. Did I even hear them? Those sounds represent a personal history, or the memory of that face that could, and probably was, completely silent.

I move into the vacuum and observe the white walls. Those from before no longer exist, I tell myself. I envision how to start painting again, one convincing first gesture, a glamorous brush stroke, and then another. Simple, if only the face would allow for it. I sit on the floor with Camila on my right side. We both stare at the space, the walls, the pale air.

"Camila, I need to paint a face."

"What face this time?"

"I don't know, everyman's face."

"Paint my face."

"No, I need to fall into the face."

"But, Teaston…"

"No, Camila."

"She is dead, Teaston."

Camila knows. Paint, canvas, brushes, they all stay outside my studio for one day and one night. An easy night—no dreams, no explanations. The day tells a different story. I reject the light as I reject people calling my name. And at the end, I turn my back on the idea of painting anything that resembles a face, not a lip contour, not the angle of a jaw, not the concealing expression of dark eyes. Finally I understand I paint amply but salvage nothing.

You bastard!

A vast space.

My past.

Where have I been?

Why would I want to remember? Let it be vast, bast, bastard, you.

You bastard!

I left Paris. Did I leave Paris? Yes. Water already existed in the river Seine. A flowing body of water that took me nowhere. I cannot tell where that nowhere lay. Did I leave Paris? My mother left me by water, her road and her escape. I swam in that river trying to reach her, but the current dragged my clumsy body away from her. I wanted to join the river, stream with the current, one body, only one body, but no. And after that I must have…

I think I painted.

Yes, motherfucker, you painted.

I painted because of the paint. Every tube of paint, when squeezed, sources a river. I painted because of the river in the paint. Going from nowhere to nowhere else in a river of magenta, or vermilion red. I dripped paint trying to go deeper. And the liquid of the paints drowned me.

Death.

No, not then, death is with me now.

Then I had the water within the colors, the water within the deep scars of the city, moving her away from me. When everything melted, when everything dripped, the colors of nothingness coalesced. Death, maybe, but I did not feel it that way.

Here comes a memory. It glides away from me. Memory, *me muero*, me more, more of me, meme, mimeme, transmitted from one mind to another. Where did it go? Where have all of them gone? My memories, my early deaths.

I concentrate and open my mind. I create an empty receptacle to collect my memories, those fugitive pieces of life. But nothing falls in, the wind most have taken away my recollections. The diaspora of my early life frightens me. I have no past ground. Do I have a ground now? Yes, my right hand digs into it. But then, what about then?

I think my fluids always felt the pull of the moon. I may have risen in springs past. But if I did, I do not remember. I could have been an idolater, an assassin of the night, a king, I could have waged war, made anonymous love, and I could have even died before. So many rooms in the house of my past, so many closed doors.

Then came the whiteness and I learned about that name of mine. How could that be my name? If I was not Teaston before how could I be Teaston now?

"Teaston."

Not at ease, tension, tension.

"Teaston."

And this old port grew from the edge of the water, like a shore, the earth tasting salt in its lips. My lips tasting nothing, for I arrived in Cassis in the unanimous night when nobody saw me. I remember looking around and marveling at the drama of the cliff, the tide, the very edge of the earth's body, and the rocks taking the spit of the sea. How I got here remains a mystery to me. I walked south, yes, but for how long? And when the morning landed, I knew I was at the edge of my body.

Yes, motherfucker.

I succumb to the vast space, my past, and the vacuity of that early nothingness. Did I have a color then? Not white, no, maybe gray, or was it purple? What thoughts did I think? Did I love? Did I fear? Had I already imagined the profile of my death?

You were nothing then, like you are nothing now, you bastard!

A winter hope of dreams...

Not closer than one hundred meters, as close as she ever gets to my studio, Her Majesty approaches. I don't even know how she reaches this far. I see her there, crawling on her knees, all bent over hiding behind a giant agave plant. I do not look. No, I will not look.

"Teaston, look this way."

"Hell, no."

She never changes her clothes, always wearing the same filthy skirt. She wants me in there, inside that skirt. Look at her, crawling like an animal. But I do not look her way, in defiance. Even with Camila next to me, she still comes to harass me.

I go into my studio, close the door, and count until three hundred. That should be enough time for her to get bored and decide to return to the port. She belongs there, if she belongs anywhere. I crack the door open and peek through the sliver of light. Her Majesty sits behind the agave with a bottle in her hands. What if she stays there all day? What if she doesn't leave? I glance at her, quickly, and see her drinking out of that bottle. Campari, maybe, she drinks it straight. She will drink until the bottle is empty, I know.

"Have a drink, Teaston."

Her Majesty lies comfortably on the ground behind the agave. She takes the bottle with her right hand and slips it under her skirt. She then pushes it rhythmically between her legs.

"Remember when…"

I do not remember anything. I close the door to avoid any sound. She should not know that I look at her, but she knows. Where is Camila when I need her? Camila, talk to me now, talk to me. Say anything you want, just talk to me. I wait for the words but only the breeze and the crackling sound of the fluorescent lights come to me. I wait for Camila's words.

Nothing.

With my shoulder I push the door just so slightly and the vertical opening shows Her Majesty horizontally on the ground.

"What a lovely day, Teaston."

"Oh, no."

Soft, softly, I close the door hoping to make no sound. Her Majesty is all ears and eyes, she anticipates my movements; I believe she hears my thoughts. And like a cat hunting, I glide towards the door on the opposite side of the house and leave the studio. I can leave this place, I can escape Her Majesty.

Camila, where are you?

When I open the southern back door, the overwhelming view of the cliff vandalizes my confidence. The promontory, green, gray, green, with a blue backdrop, reminds me of that face, the face of that woman who did what I have not done.

Camila, call me now, right now.

And my mind imagines her fall, my right hand prevents my fall, and the blood on the rocks, not my blood, the blue water ignorant of who was who, just ready to swallow whomever. And the coldness of her eyes, maybe a peaceful departure, but still looking at me before she left all behind, a little of it left with me, too much for me. The cliff seems to breathe, to take in the moist greenish air from the soil and the bluish salty air from the sea. The cliff does not care; it stands tall.

Camila, why don't you call me?

Keeping my back bent, and my head close to the ground, I dodge Her Majesty's gaze and move closer to the cliff. She cannot see me; nevertheless, I will not think too much because she may hear my thoughts. I do not think, but I am. I shift now, I think about Marcel, which confuses her, how about a thought about eating fish? The more irrelevant the thoughts, the more confused she gets.

My skull is a hard shell. It should be a sealed cavity keeping all the thoughts inside. But somehow, thoughts seep through the fissures and reach Her Majesty. She makes the best of them, learning everything about me. She can tell when I feel frustrated with my painting; she knows when I go down to the old port, when I take my boat for an escape, when Camila and I argue. I think she knows when we make love, certainly when I consider leaving Camila, she knows that. She also knows that I have been close to jumping off the cliff, that I feel driven to jump, that I do not want to look at her or sleep with her, that I fear of what she knows—she knows that.

I take small steps in the direction of the cliff, inching little by little. Her Majesty behind me, the cliff in front—twice the death. The other night I held the ground with my right hand, today I feel vulnerable; my hand may not hold the rest of me. I dodge Her Majesty's sight as the cliff touches the bottom of my feet and lies down beneath me. Who could tell that such a supple terrain, a gracious curve under your foot, a provider of majestic viewpoints, could also become the departing point of the jilted?

"Teaston, what are you thinking?"

"I think nothing."

I suffuse my fear with words to avoid her reading my mind. And with every absurd thought, thoughts like,

the force of a nymph seals the coffin,

"yes" because a "no" would

only result in a headache,

a rose was a rose then

but now we don't care,

Campari is made of the blood of smiling dwarfs

—this one will get her—

the air blows children in pieces

to a winter hope of wings

and the violet of the morning.

There, Your Majesty, think about that one.

I traverse the terrain without her knowing and the closer I get to the edge of the cliff, the more ecstatic I become. Her Majesty has no power over me. She can call me now if she wants but I will not listen. I reach the edge and smell the salty air from below. A face, and then another. All the images I attempted to paint fly over me, looking deep into my skull. I get a sense that everyone who ever was lives under the clarity of the water surface. I lean over the cliff and the ground vanishes. I venture.

A thump.

I feel the cracking of my back, my body turning and turning, some blood. But my right hand digs, as before, nails and all.

The air blowing children in pieces

to a winter hope of dreams...

Teaston, you

Camila does not know that I went to the cliff. She does not know that

I tried to jump.

Did I try to jump?

Yes.

Instead, she thinks I tripped and fell over a rock or something like that. I bet she did not see or hear Her Majesty. Her Majesty is crafty, she never says anything when Camila hovers around, and she takes good care not to be seen. Camila is so proper, so presentable, while Her Majesty looks like a bedraggled mutt. I do not think she is a real *clocharde* but she dresses the part. I will never let them see each other. No, never.

Camila takes two or three gauzes, soaks them in warm water, and wipes the mixture of dirt and blood stuck to the skin of my back. Hands of an angel. There is a gash, superficial but ugly. Another abrasion covers most of my right forearm. I reach that one but Camila insists in cleaning that one too.

Hands of an angel.

Where I lost skin, a globular yellowish substance shows, like the essence of a self, or ectoplasm. This happens when the mind and the will do not speak the same language. Like a continental divide, a platform coexisting next to another platform, but at different levels. I jumped, but my hand betrayed me again. What does my hand know that my mind seems to ignore? This right hand needs to paint his face, or her face, or the face of everyman. I visualize the image, the facial gestures, and the light within the eyes. But disconnected, my hand does not reproduce what my mind sees. But a hand cannot think. Maybe this hand belongs to someone else, attached to me in the middle of the night, or after having too many glasses of Bandol wine.

"Poor Teaston."

"Don't pity me."

"I won't."

"Then don't."

"Teaston, hold your arm up."

"Be careful with my arm and don't trust that hand."

"Teaston?"

"I fear my hand is an agent."

I decide to spend the rest of the day lazing around and keeping a minimum of awareness. Camila knows to close windows and doors when she sees me behave like a reptile. She then inspects her nursing job and feels accomplished, I think.

Under the limited light of a desktop lamp, I open a book so familiar I think I wrote it myself. The opening sentence reads something like this: "Tonight I went to the edge of the cliff." I become interested and read the first page. It resonates with something deep inside of me. But this book cannot be about me, and I could not have written it. I look at my right hand passing the pages and wonder. No, I am not going there.

"What are you reading, Teaston?"

"I'm not reading anything."

"That book you just closed."

"I don't know how to read."

"Teaston, you."

Engulfed by the body of the sea

The call of the *cigale* at night reminds me that I am alive.

I like the feeling.

Without disturbing Camila, I leave the bedroom and follow the corridor out into the open porch. There the sounds grow. The night seems foreign to me, I mistrust the strangeness of the shadows. I can be naked in the shadows, but I detest when they touch me. A certain death fills the air when the shadows coalesce. The absence of light and color, I suppose. I resolve to venture out into the night, maybe because I feel alive, or maybe because I may encounter death in a shadow. No, it will not be that way. My death will probably be a visible one, it will be next to me at high noon.

By foot I take the meandering road down to the old port. The *cigale* greet me at every turn. Yes, I am alive for the moment. As I pass near the agave plant where Her Majesty hid before, I look and confirm that she left. She took the bottle with her. She never leaves traces, the fox. With me, she flaunts it all. She can be down by the port, waiting, or simply drunk and unconscious in an alley. I heard her call me from behind the lighthouse at the mouth of the harbor. She hides very well, but I always find her. I don't want to find her, I don't even want to look her way.

I walk at a steady pace, helped by the gentle angle of decline, going by light posts, closed windows, street signs, at the same time as I rethink what being alive means. Yes, the *cigale* started everything by calling me, but now I am on my own. Descending at night, how deadly that sound. From high to low, from the top of a cliff to the bottom of the sea. A fatal trajectory or a leisurely walk?

I keep walking.

When I reach the old port in the middle of the night, I find it empty. A cat turns a corner at tremendous speed. Maybe I interrupted its vigil, or maybe it sensed something, as cats tend to do. The nocturnal waves beat on the hulls of boats and against the seawall. They sound like an anonymous crowd, giddy and placid, no one person louder than the other. The wind makes a rope flutter. No other sounds. I enter the open terrace of my customary restaurant and take a seat at my customary table. The place seems the same as in daytime, only empty and a little dead. Without Marcel to serve me, I do not get any wine. What a shame. Maybe death is like this, a familiar place without familiar people, or maybe death is a continuous sound like the sound of the sea. Or maybe death is life without its wine. At this time of the night, Camila rests deeply, and Her Majesty has no words for me. I am alone at this time. I am alive. I am Teaston. If I were many my name would be Legion. But I am one, I extend, but I am only one.

Strange how I never say my own name out loud. Everyone uses my name, they throw it at me, but I never pronounce it myself.

Let me try: "Teaston."

Sounds different from what I normally hear, graver, even harsher. I don't own my name, other people do. They use it all the time, and they may continue using it when I die, when I no longer call myself. Have I always been called Teaston? Have I always been Teaston?

"Teaston, I'm Teaston now."

That sounds almost convincing. If I called myself by another name, would it change who I am? If one day I call myself "Marcel," would I be serving Teaston a glass of wine at this table? Or, if Marcel called himself "Teaston", who would serve the two of us at this table?

"Teaston."

That was not me calling my name.

"Teaston, Teaston."

I stand up and look in all directions. Shadows and shadows. The sea lies there with all its noises but it does not have a mouth, it cannot call me. Maybe a cat? No, not really. The wind then. About a minute in alert before I sit at my table again. If someone calls me by my name, it means that such a person believes that I am Teaston. If I called myself "Teaston" in front of that person, then the belief that I am Teaston is seconded. But if both of us were confused, or simply wrong, Teaston would be a fabrication and the name just a string of letters. What would happen to the skull, hands, ears, and lungs of that person who could no longer be what we thought Teaston was? Garbage, that is all.

"Teaston."

From the sea, it comes from the sea. I rush to the seawall and look up and down the quay. The numerous boats line up one next to another, all tied together creating a bobbing constellation. No one is there. The water looms as a massive blackness at this time. A crest catches a moon ray here and there but the blackness prevails. In between the boats I look, no one.

"Teaston."

Yes, from the sea but further away. I step in front of the boat ramp and look out into the mouth of the harbor. Not a soul, just a voice.

"Teaston."

Today I am Teaston, I think I am. I shed all my clothes and enter the blackness of the sea, naked, a cold blackness that wraps my body and numbs my muscles. A few swimming strokes bring me away from the docked boats and into the openness of the harbor. What or who calls me? Am I not who I say I am?

"Teaston."

A yearning, a voice, deeper, deeper.

My body glides through the black water, stroke after stroke. The lights from the port applaud as I seek the source of my name. I reach for the sound, I reach for myself as a word. I come to this blackness because today I am Teaston. I swim against the current that forms at the mouth of the harbor, I pass the lighthouse to my left, and finally reach the open sea. The large body of water holds me without asking questions. I float on my back and barely move my arms or my legs. The waves cover and uncover my ears and the sounds become muffled and then crisp, a life rhythm.

My name is not here anymore.

My nameless body engulfed by the body of the sea.

I cannot be found

The morning light cancels the night.

Marcel arrives first in the virgin morning. He looks at me strangely because I am already at my table before he gets a chance to open the restaurant. He comes balancing a glass of wine on the little tray. I let him know that what I really need is coffee; there will be time for wine later. He brings me a cup of coffee and after laying it on the table stands in front of me, staring, as if I had something to explain. I feel his right eye poking at me.

"Why so early?"

"I really came here very late."

"Seems early to me."

"Early for today but late for yesterday."

"Will you paint today?"

"As soon as I find my name."

"Where are you looking?"

"In the sea."

Marcel knows not to ask pointed questions, but he still does, he cannot help asking. Like he cannot help the movements of his right eye. When I give him an absurd answer he stops. Like he did now. My answers seem absurd but they tell the real story. I could tell him about the sea, but his world would not change because of that. He would possibly look at me strangely, as he always does. The wine, maybe the wine now.

From Marcel's mouth, "Teaston."

"You call me Teaston?"

"What else can I call you?"

"Nothing."

"The wine, I suppose."

"Yes, the wine."

I remain at my table and watch how people start flooding the old port. The sea has shed all of its blackness and radiates with a luminous energy, the same sea that called me last night, the same sea that took me deep into its body. The Mediterranean embodies many seas, the one last night wanted to know me, this one, in the morning hours, seems indifferent. I wonder how many people the sea knows intimately, how many people live inside its body.

The walk up the hill to my studio feels less frightening, mainly because of the light, or maybe because the wine drops a veil of bliss over my face. Something changes with the light and the wine. Whatever that something, I am still the same, I think I am. I will know for sure when I reach the studio. Camila must be missing me, she gets so upset, so unnerved when I go missing for a few hours. She fears I will do something erratic, something that would change me forever. Jumping off the cliff would change me forever, but she does not know how close I have come. Camila is a good woman, and she is herself all the time. Although, when she calls me, her voice sounds strange, as if a less nurturing person had taken possession of her. But I could be distorting her words.

She is a good woman, Camila is.

When I reach the door to my studio I hesitate for a second before I fully enter into my painter's space. I walk into this room as Teaston. Who else could walk through this door, paint like I paint, make love to Camila, and harbor the questions that I harbor, but myself? Or at least, myself as Teaston. The space looks as it should, the hours of absence have not altered the way it feels to be in this room. I know Camila must be near because I sense a calming energy entering my body. I need that energy.

From Camila's mouth, "Teaston."

"Yes, please, call me."

"Where were you?"

"I went looking for my name."

"Teaston?"

"Yes, that's it."

Camila presses her face against mine and I feel her warmth. I then rest my head on her bosom. She mumbles something that I cannot understand. But whatever that is, it feels soothing. I like when she gazes at me from the corner of her eyes. In those moments she regards me as her personal Teaston, whatever I represent for her. She never questions me, and that allows me to exist next to her. She is aware I do not fully understand myself. She takes care not to break the fragile and inconclusive self of mine. I think I know Camila, I think I know her better than I know myself.

"Teaston, someone was looking for you this morning."

"I was looking for myself this morning."

"No, Teaston, someone came here looking for you."

"I cannot be found."

III

I am water

There was the time when... Again.

There was the time when I...

This is not easy.

There was the time when I behaved as if I were water.

"Camila don't respond, no comments please."

There was the time when I had a surface, and under it, a lot of me resided. Camila stares at me with that expression of disbelief. Water, like the sea, a body of water, not the water flowing from a faucet. Bodies of water extend from shore to shore. How difficult is it to imagine water like that? During that time, things floated on me and the air made ripples on my skin.

Camila sits next to me ready to listen. I know she is ready because she tilts her head sideways and half closes her eyes. That does not mean she believes what I tell her.

There was a time when I was water.

Camila seems so eager to believe the premise. Her readiness disarms me. She is Camila, and she could listen to what I have to say. But at the same time she can dismiss me. Camila, she is. But I still ask her to sit close to me and listen to my story of water. This, a story I do not know how to tell.

I.

I am.

I am water, a restless fluid, a voluminous self that goes as deep as the inverted mountains underneath the sea. My body does not hold me; it liberates itself unto gutters. I do not run, I flow. And my body joins with the creeks, the rivers, the seas. I am like a drip, a drip that slides until it crashes making a puddle at the end. I am water and I should dribble down the cliff and join with the sea below.

I am not a tangible Teaston.

I am oceanic.

We stay close to each other for some time, grabbing each other's fingers. I think of the night before and she thinks of something else. Together, we think of each other's thoughts without knowing what those thoughts could be. But, can she tell what my thoughts are? Sometimes I think she can, like Her Majesty. Well, she is not at all like Her Majesty. One of her hands comes to rest on my shoulder, a caress maybe.

Yes, a caress.

Then she squeezes my right hand. That hand of mine, the one that keeps on holding the ground. I look at Camila and she appears so natural, unaware of the saving grit of my right hand. She expects me to be Teaston, the painter, the one who will not be water, the one who will be reasonable. Logical, even. Her acceptance of my stories, of myself, devastates me.

"Teaston, you."

"Yes, me, but..."

I stand and grab Camila's hand and ask her to follow me. She never says "No." We step out of the studio and I lead the way toward the cliff. Camila never goes near the cliff. She likes the view of the sea but from a secure place, not from the edge. Something happened to her when she was little, I am sure. She knows where I am heading, and the closer we get to the cliff, the harder she squeezes my hand. I have taken Camila everywhere around Cassis, but never to the cliff.

"Teaston, why go there?"

"We can admire the sea."

"I can see it from here."

"It's not the same."

The promontory ahead implies emptiness. Birds spread their wings and hold them open against the air. Other than the birds in the sky, there is nobody at the edge of the cliff. We arrive and sit on the ground. Camila leans against me, turning her face away from the sea. Her body feels stiff and she does not say anything for a while. The openness in front of me grows grand, and I notice the white caps forming on the surface of the sea.

When I rest my head on her bosom, I fear little. I sense the need to belong, to join the sea, but not the need to lose myself.

"Teaston, is this where you saw her?"

"Yes, this is where I saw her face."

"Why did she jump?"

"I don't know."

Camila does not dare to look into the precipice. She lays the weight of her head over my shoulder, but continues looking out into the mountains, away from the sea. Camila loves life, and she does not delve into issues of death. She knows many other things, but not much about death. Maybe she tries to forget the immediacy of death, like most people do.

"Camila, look at the sea."

"No."

"Look at the vastness."

"Teaston, why do you bring me here?"

"I want you to find me."

"I know where you are."

"I'm here, but I'm also at the bottom of the cliff. I'm water."

"Teaston."

"I lie down and my body reaches Africa."

"Let's go back, Teaston."

Camila can always tell when I begin to lose myself. That fascinates me, her ability to know when I am coming apart. In her presence, I feel capable of regarding myself, that vast sea below. I walk away from the cliff as if walking away from a funeral. For Camila this is different, she has no connection to the cliff, she fears it in a more logical way, the basic fear of falling. For me, the cliff represents the edge, the threshold, a line between two selves.

"Camila, I'm water."

People are finding me

Five days, an intemperate amount of time, enough to forget the details of a face and to drink Bandol in excess. Five days after first meeting the phenomenon, Phillipy knocks at the door of my studio and waits for my response. I do not answer, hoping he will turn around and go away. In remain silent. Why do I have to attend to Marcel's son? He said Phillipy was his son. Yes. What about his mother? Why is she not caring for him? He attacks the door again and the knocks bounce inside my head like lost words in a cave. I ask Camila to open the door pretending I have no idea who is knocking, but knowing very well that Phillipy must be out there prepared to take my world as his.

"A young man, Phillipy or something, is asking for you."

"I know."

"Teaston, he looks…"

"I know."

I brace for the worst and lead Phillipy inside my studio. Carrying a black leather bag, he enters with confidence, as if he were familiar with the place. He looks everywhere except at me. Opening his bag, he takes out two or three brushes, tubes of oil paint, rags, linseed oil, and the most ridiculous oversized red painter's hat. He readies himself and waits for something to happen.

"Are you here to paint or to watch me paint?"

"You're Teaston."

"Yes, and you're Phillipy."

"Phillipy is here to watch Teaston paint. He's waiting."

I move around the studio considering how to approach everyman's face today. Not only do I have to contend with my doubts and difficulties, I also have to deal with the man/child who seems eager to emulate my efforts. He watches as I move about the studio. But he does not look directly at me; instead, he turns his face away and tracks my movements from the corner of his eyes. Not a word he utters.

How do I do this? Why do I do this? In all likelihood, I will not paint anyone's face today. I will probably make an attempt, an insignificant gesture at best. And this man, or child, will be my witness. There he waits, ready for a display of my virtuosity. I start by spreading a field of yellow on top of the multiple layers of paint that cover the veteran canvas. The face, everyman's, or her face, before the fall. I draw a line, then another. I shape a round form of darkness by means of black and red. My hand, my right hand, spreads vivid colors, draws dark lines, and lies unanimously. Phillipy looks directly at my hand as it shapes forms that will not last into the evening. I predict that nothing will survive after the end of the session. I paint to erase, I paint to cover the faces that show me who I am.

The play of colors and lines goes on for a while. Phillipy is absorbed by the continuous evolution of the images. He seems exited. He gesticulates in strange ways, his hands fluttering in front of his face.

"Is Teaston painting a man or a woman?"

"I don't know."

"Is Teaston painting a girl?"

"I don't know how to paint."

"But Marcel said Teaston is a painter."

"Your father?"

"Yes, Marcel said Teaston is a painter."

"I'm trying to paint a face."

"Teaston is painting a face."

"I think I'm painting a face."

"Is that a face, Teaston?"

"No, this is my fiasco."

"Teaston, paint a face."

"Phillipy, I cannot paint a face now."

"Phillipy, paint a face. Paint a face, Phillipy."

He takes his brushes and starts to paint at a vertiginous speed in his own white canvas. He mixes colors, makes shadows, smudges edges, intensifies angles, and draws eyes, a nose, ears, neck, lips, and many layers of hair. Phillipy stares at the canvas with an intensity I have never seen. He seems furious, but no grunt or growl comes out of his mouth. He paints as Marcel promised, in a talented way. Laboring for a long while, entranced, Phillipy creates a cryptic yet intimate image.

"Phillipy painted this face."

"Who's this?"

"This is Teaston."

I look at the face on the canvas and recognize a smirk, and a small downturn of the left eye, a vacancy all too familiar. I do not want to recognize myself, not in the painting of this man, child, or whatever. But I see myself and I know something about me can be painted, represented, even by a creature like Phillipy. I prepare a batch of white-grayish paint and give it to Phillipy who stares at the paint not knowing what to do.

"Paint it over with this."

"If Phillipy paints it over, the face will be gone."

"I know."

"Paint it over?"

"Yes, cover the whole thing."

"But Teaston is a painter."

"This is how we're painting today."

Was that my face? My face, me. Now covered.

I ask Phillipy to leave the studio and return home to Marcel. This encounter with myself finds me naked, exposed. Like turning a corner and coming face to face with the self, how menacing.

Camila, where are you? Camila come here.

People are finding me.

I think I am

At the restaurant, while sitting at my table, I watch a short man and a tall bearded man stare at me and speak to each other. I turn around and ask Marcel for another glass of Bandol, making sure only the back of my neck stays exposed. I do not look their way. The wine tastes just as it should, except for the drops of fear that accentuate the tannins. Slowly, with the lethargy of a lizard, I turn my face and look in the direction where the two men were standing before.

Nobody.

I breathe.

Two men stared at me. No one there now. They did not talk to me, not a word—just a suspicious stare.

Today Marcel seems more hectic than usual. He runs to the bar, to a table, to the kitchen, back to another table. His right eye becomes frenetic. I see it jumping everywhere, the arteries all red, a vitreous fury threatening to come loose from its socket. He accommodates people wherever he can and nobody gets what they wish soon enough. I take my feet off the empty chair opposite to mine; somebody may need it. I hold on to my table but the chair I donate to the crowd. Next to me a fat lonely man stands up from his aching chair and leaves the restaurant. Immediately, the two men that were spying on me materialize out of nowhere, and occupy the table next to mine. Where they come from, I do not know. Why they choose this particular table, I can only guess. True, there are no other empty tables in the restaurant, but this one is right next to mine.

The short man sits on the suffering chair previously vacated by the fat man. The bearded one turns my way and asks if he could take the empty chair in front of me. I make an ambiguous gesture, which he understands as an affirmation, for he takes the chair and sits next to the short man. The sun sets now, slowly, and the fierce red light makes their faces petrifying.

The two men seem anxious, jittery, filled with uneasiness. They share a few words between themselves and gaze at me from the corner of their eyes. They study the menu and call for Marcel, who looks at everything and everyone with his feverish eye. I also signal to Marcel with the hope that he will come to my table before he attends to these two strange men. But Marcel knows what I usually want, and without asking, he brings another glass of Bandol and quickly turns to the two men and takes their order.

The two men speak in a low tone of voice, as if hiding their words from me. I watch their lips, trying to guess what they say. The short man opens his mouth and pulls his jaw down and slightly back after which his lower lip touches the bottom of his upper teeth.

"Cliff," he must be saying "cliff."

The bearded man turns his head a few degrees in my direction, just enough to catch a glimpse of me. I do not look his way. At that time Marcel, arrives balancing a tray with their order. He places two bottles of beer on their table and sticks the bill under the ashtray to keep it from flying away. Before Marcel has a chance to run back to the kitchen, the short man talks to him in a strange accent.

"Have you heard about a woman that was pushed from the cliff not too long ago?"

"A woman jumped from the cliff, I think."

"Jumped?"

"I believe so."

"You believe so."

An experienced waiter, Marcel cuts the conversation short, collects a few empty glasses, and returns to the bar. From the distance, I notice his right eye focusing on me for a few unblinking seconds.

In one long gulp I finish the wine in my glass, stand with my back towards the two men, and walk out of the restaurant into the mass of people parading down the quay. These men are after me. They are finding me. I move fast among the crowd gaining distance from them, from the fear.

Many unknown faces turn my way, as if they knew something about me, something I do not even know myself. I sit at the seawall and try to disappear by ignoring the faces and peering into the clear water. The water lies here for me; it knows me well. I observe how the wind makes ripples on the surface and I feel my skin wrinkling as well. I could live immersed here, in water.

"Teaston."

"Why now?"

"Teaston."

I turn and find Her Majesty sitting on the bow of one of the boats tied to the seawall. She waves at me with her usual flair. The breeze plays with her disarrayed hair and her loose dress. I refuse to look her way.

"Look at me, Teaston."

"No."

"Look at me."

Her Majesty pulls her dress up, extends her legs, and spreads them as wide as she can. Her vagina assaults me.

"Let's go sailing, Teaston."

"I'm not going into the sea with you."

"Well, you won't go into the sea alone, will you?"

"Don't talk about the sea."

"Come, sail into me."

I look at the crowd behind me and find no trace of the two men. But in front of me is Her Majesty with her incredible sense of timing and location. She always finds me. I try to avoid her at all costs but she finds me. She found me in the midst of whiteness, I did not look for her; she found me. And when I could not tell what was real or who was real, when the only light around me was a white light, her lips emerged and started calling me. And wherever I go she finds me there, and she lures me. I could join her and sail into the sea, into the white mist, certain that she will trap me between her legs. There, between her legs, I would disappear into whiteness again. Her Majesty, the Queen of Whiteness. I cannot return to that space where my thoughts run unbridled, where everything inside my mind needs to go out, and everything outside rushes in, where nothing is what it seems to be, where confusion reigns supreme, where the bug of whiteness weakens my mind.

I am Teaston now.

I think I am.

She fills me

Camila spends long hours by herself. She leaves in the morning not carrying much, just a bottle of water and her old and beaten binoculars. She steps out of the studio by the southern door, that way the sun shines on her. She never tells me what she explores on those long walks. Sometimes, she comes unannounced to my table at the port. Then I know she is meandering around town. But other times she loses herself around the cliff, or by the shore. She doesn't like to swim; the sea is not her realm. But she goes everywhere else, alone and happy. Camila, I think, lives a happy life.

Unlike me, Camila is oblivious of people. Sometimes I see someone or another look my way, or talk in whispers as I go by. But she has no problem ignoring them. I do not think she even notices them at all. I would never talk to her about this. It would only make her worry about things she does not need to worry about. She does her best with Her Majesty. Even when Her Majesty reaches the peak of her impertinence, Camila ignores her completely; she acts as if she did not exist. I think that explains why Her Majesty does not dare coming to my studio. She knows Camila exists there and hates being ignored.

She is secretive, Camila is, an endearing quality of hers. I only know so much about her. She returns the favor by not asking about the whiteness or any other time of my life. I know the Camila that lies next to me at this time, the one who offers me her bosom, I imagine others exixt, but I do not want to know them.

When she comes back from her walks, at the end of the day, she usually finds me laboring over incomplete faces. She sits next to me because she knows my distress. She says my name. She calls me "Teaston." Sometimes I resist and answer with an abrupt "No" when what I want to say is "Yes."

One day she came from one of her long walks and admired my painting, unfinished as usual, and with her light spirit, a spirit that grounds me, she asked me to explain what I painted. I could not say. I said the painting was incomplete, and that it would disappear by the end of the day. Her lips formed a tender smile.

She fills me.

This is you

"And Phillipy?"

"He's not here."

"Better. He's strange."

"He painted my portrait."

"Did you pose for that?"

"No, he painted it from memory."

"Where's the portrait?"

"He covered it with paint, my image is gone."

"Did it look like you?"

"I don't know how I look."

"Teaston."

"Whatever he painted wasn't me."

"Did he get upset with you?"

"There's no way of telling. I cannot tell what he thinks. He just painted me and I wasn't going to look at myself. I hate him for painting me."

"But Teaston, he's just a…"

"He can sense it, he knows I'm nothing."

Phillipy may know more than he reveals. He cannot hold a conversation, but he seems keenly aware of the conversations of others. I never find him at the restaurant when I go there to speak with Marcel. But somehow, I believe he knows everything we talk about.

He returns today, Phillipy, armed with more brushes and an array of paint tubes. He enters my studio without greeting me, sets a blank canvas on a disjointed easel, and just stands there, waiting for me. I watch him, and he knows that I am watching him, but he says nothing.

"Good morning, Phillipy."

"Yes, the morning is good."

Once he hears my voice, Phillipy starts painting with speed and determination. He opens one paint tube after another, mixes colors, and layers the various pigments creating a figure out of the whiteness of the canvas. When he paints, Phillipy sticks his tongue out the side of his mouth, in pure concentration, as if the tongue was directing the brush strokes. Energy pours out of his forehead in the form of sweat, and nothing stops him. A good hour goes by and Phillipy does not slow down. He paints from memory, no photographs, no sketches, just an image that resides in his mind. I stand behind him and get completely absorbed by the spectacle of this man/child painting with such urgency. I am aware that he is aware of me, but his face does not reveal the awareness. I watch Phillipy jabbing and stroking the canvas. He is not tentative; he applies every brush with resolve, as if he knew where all lines and shapes belong.

He becomes aware of me.

"Phillipy is painting."

This unrequested assertion seems to propel him to a faster pace and bolder color combinations.

"Phillipy will stop painting when he's finished."

"Are you painting your father?"

"Phillipy isn't painting Marcel."

"How about your mother?"

"Phillipy cannot paint his mother."

"Why not?"

"Phillipy cannot paint his mother."

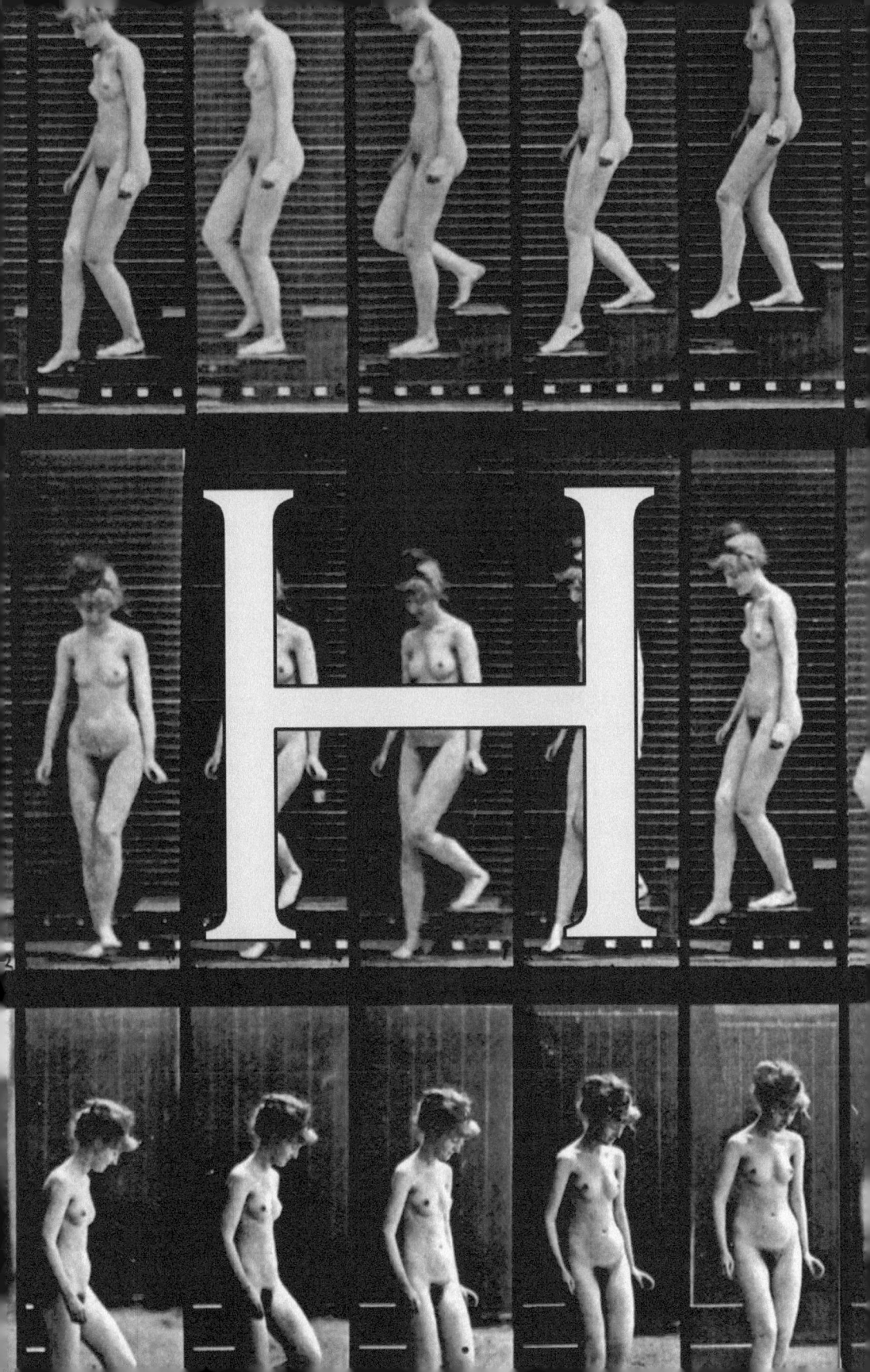

"Is she pretty?"

"Phillipy cannot paint his mother. Three times, that's it."

I try to catch a glimpse of what he paints but he hovers all over the canvas and does not let me see his progress. I want to call his attention, make him slow down, perhaps, have longer conversations with him. But Phillipy sails into his own world, and my presence at this point seems irrelevant to him. Why did I agree to this arrangement? Marcel should take care of this man/child by himself.

"Teaston, this is you."

I push Phillipy to the side and confront what he painted all morning. All the mixed colors produce a white-grayish tonality that covers the entire canvas. There is no discernible face, there is nothing.

"Teaston, this is you."

Other faces call me

The son of the mayor, Lucio, had a delicate face, like an angel—sharp angles, oblong eyes, and a classic Greek nose. We depict angels as beautiful creatures; we need them to be beautiful. Otherwise, how could we explain their privileged position? I saw his face before the rocks disfigured him. He played with his soccer teammates, testing the limit, tiptoeing at the edge of the cliff. On a violent push and pull, he was pushed, but there was no pull. I saw his face. And that was all I told the *gendarmes* when they asked me about his fall. I saw his face, I said then. His friends said he jumped off the cliff by himself, that he wanted to fly, they said.

I can still see his face. No desire to end anything, no wanting to fly; I only see a startled expression. That is the face I saw, but the *gendarmes* did not want to hear about it. After all, their kids play soccer with all other kids and no one is responsible for anyone's death. This I know well. The *gendarmes* installed a yellow tape with the word *"ATTENTION"* printed in bold letters. The warning kept people away from the cliff for a while until the strong winds tore it appart.

When Lucio's face lands on my lap, I try to paint him. He does not have everyman's face; he has the face of the forgotten. I take a Renaissance approach, depicting him in a diaphanous light, like an angel, without much resemblance to the face I actually saw. I layer sepia, viridian and burnt umber, some pewter, creating a luminous sfumato, veiling the space between him and me. Lucio never knew himself in this light, how could he? Camila likes his image but I never tell her who Lucio really is. She thinks I am painting a cherub, a little angel.

When the *gendarmes* came to interrogate me about Lucio, I turned the picture around. I did not want to trouble him. Lucio told me once he despised the *gendarmes*, and I understood him. The *gendarmes* never returned, at least not to ask about Lucio, and he was happy. He is happy now, I think, although I have not painted him lately. I try to paint him sometimes, but the face of the olive woman comes to my brushes and steers me away from him.

Lucio has an endearing voice, part song and part whisper. When Camila comes into the studio, he remains quiet; he listens as I speak with her but offers no comment. Once the studio becomes silent again, he murmurs with every stroke of the brush. I change tonalities, add one layer of paint after another, but still saving his image. That makes him happy. Lucio knows that I must make him disappear at the end of the day, and when I start gradually covering his image, the veil growing thicker, he calls me "Teaston." I know he wants to stay, but other faces call me.

I'm now

Today follows a long night.

Too many empty hours looking out to the sea. Nothing there. Too many hours ahead of me with no certainty there will be anything there either. I fear these days; these are the ones that precede the tempting nights. I do not need to go to the cliff tonight, but the impulse to go to the edge and sense the void will arise—I know it will. Camila sleeps next to me unaware of what I fear. Maybe when she wakes up she will sense something. Camila knows, most times.

I remain calm.

I avoid wakening her. Long, long, Camila should sleep as long as possible. It prevents the day from starting, from unleashing the emptiness I anticipate. The night, now, is far. This time subsists between two parentheses, between two blades. I cannot move or she would awake, I cannot jump from bed for I would fall into the emptiness, I cannot be Teaston. Well, even if I were Teaston, there would still be emptiness. This is a time to exist as another.

Camila sighs as if she is ready to join the day. I watch her closely. She turns around, pulls the covers towards her, fixes the pillow, and with a wandering hand, finds me. I do not move. She strokes my leg and mumbles something. She turns around without opening her eyes.

The day has begun. There is no hiding place for me now. From this instant, I will need to solve the emptiness, I will need to paint a face, and I will need to fight my urge to jump.

I remain quiet, pretending I am dead asleep—dead I am, almost, but not asleep. Camila caresses my face with the back of her fingers and leaves her hand resting on top of my chest. I can support the weight of her hand, but not the weight of her expectations. She wants me to be a painter who creates something significant. I can paint, I know I can, but I need to paint the faces that call me. I wish I did not have to paint them, but their insistence is brutal, they call me and demand a rendition.

Quiet, quiet, I remain.

Her breathing softens, her face seems content. Camila, do not wake up now, let me look at you in this marvelous instant when you rest and I wonder. Only a brief moment. You will soon open your eyes and kiss me, but a question will accompany that kiss—what are you painting today?

Today I will paint the face of the olive woman who abandoned me there at the edge of the cliff. I do not want to join her, for if I were to jump, I would do it alone.

No Camila, no… I will not jump today.

I see how your eyes move frantically under your closed eyelids. You are dreaming Camila. I hope you dream about another time, not today, today has already started and offers nothing. There are many more days to dream about, avoid this one. I wish I could avoid it, but I am already awake and the day takes shape in front of me. The worst time, the morning is, when all possibilities are still alive, when uncertainty reaches its peak, the morning, the gravest of times. Camila, do not open your eyes. There is really nothing to regard.

The morning is still quiet.

Her Majesty, absent now, does not come at this time or to this place, she simply ignores me in moments like this. Lucio probably dreams at this time. Only Camila can reach me now, but she remains asleep. This feels as pure as this world will ever feel. I have myself all to myself, and those who call on me are nowhere around. I breathe a clean air, uncontaminated by the words of others. At this time only possibilities exist, daunting, yes, but nothing more. Without the words of others, or the faces I paint, this morning is as personal and mine as ever. I should bow to this morning and sacrifice one of my souls to it. I should stay silent and not move, to keep it alive. I should just be Teaston, now.

The gravest of times.

Camila turns towards me and slowly opens her eyes. She seems to look at me but she could be looking at a face in her dreams. Her smile is soft, like the smile of people who do not fear the day. She hugs me, pressing my head against her bare chest. She presses hard, as if wanting to give life. When she lets me go I can breathe again.

"Teaston, you are here."

"I'm now."

Your mind is elsewhere

Marcel seems saddled by a heavy load today, or at least, troubled. His fluttering right eye, half covered by his eyelid, does not move as usual, it even appears misty. The customers have to call him twice before he takes their order or prepares their bill. He brings me a glass of wine and barely acknowledges my presence. I follow his movements and try to interpret his expression. But Marcel does not talk to me long enough; I cannot tell what burdens him.

He then comes around, sits at my table, and faces me. He has never sat at my table before. At the restaurant he is Marcel, the waiter, not a friend. He looks at me for a long time. His right eye seems deadened. I sip some wine and wait for Marcel to speak. But he does not say anything; he just stares at me. A young couple sitting two tables over to my left tries to get his attention, but he continues to look at me in silence. I think I hear him say, "Please, Teaston," but he does not move his lips. I have another sip of wine and wait until he decides to speak.

Now that he faces me, I realize his right eye never blinks. There is no rest for that eye. Maybe he sleeps with that eye open. I struggle to interpret his expression, sad maybe, betrayed, or perhaps empty. Today he seems like a beaten man. Ten minutes have passed and Marcel has not moved or said a word. Marcel may be dying.

"Yes, Marcel?"

No answer. Actually, not even a sign that he hears me. Marcel ignores my words, the calls from the customers. Time. He ignores time. This reminds me of the whiteness, the time when nothing happened, and when it did, I did not care. But Marcel has never gone to the whiteness, not that I am aware. The oddity of his frozen presence and his silence makes me think...

"Teaston, come sit with me."

"This is not possible."

At the bar, Her Majesty waves at me. She wears an obscenely short

skirt and has a drink in her hand. She does not care about Marcel; she does not realize that he is disintegrating right in front of me. I turn my back to her and face Marcel. He is not here, so it seems.

"Teaston, look at me."

"No, I will not."

But I do. And there she is, Her Majesty, kneeling on the stool, resting her elbows on the counter, mooning me. But nobody notices the spectacle. People keep eating and drinking. I ignore her, I ignore her call, but I am disturbed by her lewdness. She likes to put me in this kind of situation. Her Majesty knows when to strike, she knows.

"Teaston."

I feel Marcel's strong hand shaking me. He reaches from across my table and seems alarmed, his right eye protruding with intensity.

From Marcel's mouth, "You scared me, I thought you died here."

From my mouth, "What?"

From Marcel's mouth, "You didn't answer."

From my mouth, "I didn't answer what?"

From Marcel's mouth, "I've been calling you and trying to get your attention."

From my mouth, "I have been here."

From Marcel's mouth, "No, Teaston. Your mind is elsewhere."

Drunken sailor

Not a word.

Not to Camila, as I leave before her morning meanderings. Not a word to Phillipy as I pass him on my way down, his way up to my studio. Not a word to myself because I don't need to convince myself.

I dodge.

I avoid spoken words.

My little boat receives me in silence and takes my weight, my volume, the hull serving as a barrier between the sea and myself. My boat forces its ribs and spine against the sea creating a concave space to hold me. I am dry, and I am happy. After letting go of the lines, I hoist the main sail, pull in the jib, and head for open water. There is turbulence at the mouth of the harbor like there is turbulence in my mind.

At a steady pace, I sail away from the shore, the solid ground that fails to bind me. I need to be away from people, from their inquisitive eyes, from their piercing voices. And the wind does the favor, it pushes me along, and I am happy. The buildings become smaller and the shoreline becomes longer, the sky stays the same, ample, supreme over the town of Cassis. How this town arrived in my life, I cannot remember. I wonder if the town noticed when I arrived, from the north I presume, maybe naked, or exposed. More questions than answers. I heave to and let the boat drift at will, floating in the swelling sea. Now my hands are free to hold my head and my thoughts.

A seagull flies white above me, screaming or laughing. I cannot tell. It holds out its wide wings, maneuvering on top of my boat, waiting for something to happen. There is a lot of whiteness to the seagull, and that makes me think that I am unwell. I float away from people, to avoid thinking of my time in whiteness. I stand by the stern and watch the waves crash against the boat. And at the count of one, not even three, I let my body fall into the water.

Silence surrounds me, no voices, no seagulls laughing, no calling from Her Majesty, no tender words from Camila, no faces demanding rendering, nothingness; or quite the contrary—eminence, wholeness, the entirety of myself.

Water.

I am water.

Submerged into myself feels natural, a blending of sorts. The tempest brews on the surface where the air and the sky meet my body. The violence. I arch and crest when the wind pushes me. Like an angry bastard I spit white foam. I have to go deep, deeper. And thrashing with arms and legs, I part the waters. Floating inside myself, the train of thoughts stops, and I join the deep silent currents.

No violence, only a profound peace.

I stay submerged for what seems a long time, in my essence, I suppose, until numbness takes a hold of my limbs and the natural buoyancy of my body propels me to the surface. I bob with the waves until I manage to grab the stanchion line, climb up, and throw my body into the drifting boat. The seagull laughs at me as if I were a drunken sailor.

Painted over him

Phillipy refers to himself in third person, as if existing as a separate entity from his very self. I find that habit interesting, a sport of sorts, a way of explaining one's actions from a distance. I wonder if he considers himself more than one person. When I ask him that question, he just looks at me and says that Phillipy does not understand what I am asking. He is young, but not so young, and not too old either. Not an adolescent, not and adult, part child, but part ancient as well.

I see him now, Phillipy, his rapid brush strokes creating the image of a boy. I get close to him and look at the canvas while he continues painting at a feverish pace. An angelic face stares at me. Lucio? Yes... Lucio. I step back.

"Phillipy, what exactly are you painting?"

"Phillipy is painting a young boy."

"Who is it?"

"Teaston knows him."

I see Lucio's familiar image, with the same eyes, the same mouth, and the same falling expression. He resembles my own painting; better yet, he is my own painting. The little death, the cherub that comes to me, comes to Phillipy as well. I wonder if he knows him as Lucio, or if he knows him

only as a dead stranger. Do these images talk to each other? Does Lucio know Phillipy as a first or a third person?" The little death, Lucio, why does he show his face to others?

I step back and wait for Lucio to speak to me, but he stays very quiet, he does not dare to say a word, he seems frightened by Phillipy, even though Phillipy is the one who brings him to life this morning. Lucio stays portrayed and silent. For Phillipy, this means nothing, for he has never heard Lucio speak, I think. Can he sense the boy's tragic death?

Lucio keeps staring at me from the depth of Phillipy's canvas. He wants to talk, I can tell, because he wears it on his face, an acknowledgement that he is born from the hand of another painter. But his image seems real, accurate, so he has no other alternative but to exist. I can regard this Lucio as an apocryphal being, but he is as real as the Lucio I paint myself. At this moment, Lucio only exists if a painterly hand brings him into being. It could be my hand, or Phillipy's hand, or any other hand. I am not sure if Lucio is calling Phillipy or if he is calling me to come into being.

I let Phillipy finish the painting. He begins to store all his materials, putting the oil tubes away, cleaning his brushes, and picking up rags from the floor. He seems happy, Phillipy does. And before he turns away to exit my studio, I ask him to show me the portrait of Lucio. He looks at me with a strange expression. Clearly, he does not know who Lucio is. I ask him if he knows what he just painted. Phillipy seems puzzled by my question.

"I painted what Teaston would've painted."

"But, how do you know what I would've painted?"

"Phillipy doesn't know."

"Why did you paint that young boy?"

"Because the cherub needs to talk."

Lucio needs to talk, I know, but how does Phillipy know that? He painted Lucio without knowing that, at times, I also paint him. But I am certain Phillipy does not know Lucio in the way I know him. But, do I know him? I only know he did not want to jump, that his fall could have been prevented.

I know he needs me to paint him because that brings him alive.

The little death, what is so little about Lucio's death. Maybe Phillipy sees him as a little person, vulnerable, owning a simple and small death—a little death. How could I know if the death assigned to me is appropriate? Would Phillipy think of Marcel's future death as little or grand? Would he care? And if I were to jump from that cliff, would Phillipy say my death was larger? To Phillipy, the little death of Lucio does not exist.

Phillipy starts pacing back and forth, anxious to leave for the day. I tell him to show me the little death. And when he uncovers the canvas, Lucio's image is no longer there; other colors and shades cover him, silencing him.

"What happened to the young boy?"

"He's dead."

"Do you know his face?"

"Teaston knows his face."

"Does he talk to you?"

"He doesn't talk to Phillipy, no, he doesn't."

"Why did you paint over him?"

"I didn't. Teaston painted over him."

What is a person?

Before Camila, before the whiteness, many people desired me. They wanted to speak to me, be close to me, and touch me. I had no fears. I painted many faces then, but only the ones that intrigued me. And many faces wanted to intrigue me—the self-appointed aristocrats, celebrities, other artists, people who thought highly of themselves. They offered money, and sometimes sex. But money and sex have no face. I did not hesitate when painting a face that lured me. The brush strokes found their way into the canvas, just like when Phillipy paints. But without that lure, I refused to paint.

People thought I was painting them, but in some twisted way, I was painting myself. In all those faces I found an angle that revealed a piece of me. I painted it. Distorted. Those faces were all distorted. A face breaks apart when it dies to be more than itself. I did not find myself in others; others wanted to find themselves in me. And they paid me for that—they paid a lot.

I was never alone. One face came into my studio in the Marais, then another. They did not come to pose; they just looked at me while I looked at them. Later, I would paint the worthy ones from memory. The same faces came back to my studio hoping to find their image on the unlikely mirror of the canvas. If they recognized something of themselves amidst the distortion, they were happy, if they did not see themselves, they were hopeful they were there, somehow.

I infiltrated every one of my paintings. A part of me could be found in a shadow, a line, certain expression, and absence sometimes. But I was always there, unbeknownst to the person portrayed. And when a portrait left my studio, a part of me left with it. I did not lose myself in this way, I was not spent—I learned to be everywhere.

But that happened before the whiteness, a time when every voice I heard was anchored. So different today. No one parades into my studio; no one offers money or sex. Well, Her Majesty does, but I am not sure about her. I see a part of myself in Lucio's face, in the face of the olive woman. But when I try to paint them, I cannot find me, I lose myself in them, I cease to exist in them—I am not distinguishable from them. That forces me to desecrate them. By painting over them I make the fractional image vanish. I feel like water in those moments, fluid, immersing what is left of me into the waters of another.

A painter paints; a painter finds the world in his paintings. I try to find myself in my paintings, but I fail to find Teaston in my paintings. And Teaston may not be there to be painted, rendered as a concrete being, or even as a detail, a line or a shadow of another being. Teaston may be water, a fluid that escapes capture. I speak like Phillipy now, as if Teaston were a person separate from my own self. Could Teaston and I exist as separate beings at the same time?

Are we the same person?

What is a person?

By the sea

I sit at my table, with a glass of Bandol in my hand, while trying to keep my thoughts in order, when the mayor plops himself in the empty chair next to me and arches his back. His extensive abdomen glows. I know who he is. In this small town everyone knows who the thieves are.

I ignore him and keep drinking my wine while looking at the old port. Marcel comes to the table and asks the mayor what he wants to drink. He seems composed, Marcel does, as he knows the mayor well.

"I'll have whatever Teaston is having."

I am having ideas of suicide, a sense that my thoughts are derailed, and fear that all the colors will close on me. He cannot have that. No…

"You cannot have what I'm having."

"*Monsieur* Teaston, I mean no offence to you."

"That's not my name."

"I must be confused. Aren't you the painter who lives up by the cliff?"

"Yes, I live up there, and I paint."

"Then, so…"

"And who are you?"

"Oh, excuse my imprudence. I thought you knew who I am. My name is Alain Girard, Mayor of Cassis."

He stretches his hand out over the table piercing my space. I do not reach for it; instead, I have a sip of my wine and study the lines composing his rotund face. No angelical qualities. And as he starts to pull his hand away, I grab it.

"An honor to meet you."

Marcel returns with a glass of Bandol and a disturbed expression on his face. He places the glass on the table, and before he can say a word, his whole body becomes tense and rigid. I cannot tell what he thinks, but I sense he knows what my mind harbors.

From Marcel's mouth, "This is the painter that I spoke about."

From Girard's mouth, "Yes, you said he's been very kind to Phillipy."

From Marcel's mouth, "Phillipy has learned a lot from him."

From my mouth, "He's a very talented student."

From Girard's mouth, "He painted my dead Lucio."

Your dead son? He loves to go to your studio. Maybe he does. Lucio is my dead son. I don't know your son. He's dead, but you saw him before he fell. Why did Lucio die? Phillipy paints angels. Where is the painting? I only saw his face. Who painted Lucio? Cherubs and angels, beautiful paintings. I don't know. *Monsieur* Teaston.

That is not my name.

Bandol, another Bandol. Did you paint his face? I only paint in white. What? Phillipy painted a large sea with white foam at the shore. I need to go. Where is the painting? In the white foam, by the sea.

There is only whiteness

She takes me by the hand, Camila does, and pulls me away from the studio.

"Teaston, you will not paint today."

I need to paint and she knows. But she drags me away in this unimportant morning. I agree to follow her. Camila never says much about herself. I have not entered all the rooms in her mind. But when she opens one of those rooms and lets me in, I marvel at the spectacle.

No, Camila, please… Close your mind.

I see in her what I saw before. No, not the scars.

She has many special places she visits during her extended walks. To other people they seem ordinary places, but for Camila, they have an intimate meaning.

We follow a path away from the houses, rounding the cliff, leading all the way down to the sea. I never take this path because it offers an uneasy view of the cliff. From below, the cliff threatens in a monstrous way. Camila knows I would not come this way on my own. She continues to lead me and I follow her in silence.

For Camila, the world is open, she moves with ease over any land, through any air, unperturbed. I have never seen her afraid, never, for she goes on her lengthy walks to conquer the world. She knows my world is smaller, more fragile. I do not want a larger world than the one I have. Even this one feels wobbly.

"Teaston, don't look up."

"No, I won't."

No, I will not confront the cliff. I will only look at the path in front of me, at Camila's silhouette and at her every step. She knows where she goes and the reason for taking me there. I expect to know soon. We arrive at a rocky headland at the foot of the cliff. Here the waves crash against the rocks sending salty spray everywhere. Camila sits on the rocks and pulls me next to her. She sizes up the vastness and does not say a word. I remain quiet knowing the sea lies just below, so much of me there.

"I found death here."

"What, Camila?"

"I've walked all over these rocks many times, but here's where I found death."

"What's dead here?"

"I don't know, that's why I brought you here, maybe you know."

"No, I don't."

"The woman who fell from the cliff, you saw her."

"I saw her face."

"How did she die?"

"She drowned."

No, she did not drown, she died here first, and then the sea claimed the rest of her. Her face was probably deformed after impacting the rocks. The face I fail to paint died here. Without a body, who would know? I examine the rocks around me, looking for a trace of her, an imprint on the rocks. But the sea spray washes everything, except the presence of death, a presence Camila detects but does not understand.

"She's here, Teaston, her death is here."

"No, she's somewhere else."

"I can feel…"

"Camila, she's part of the sea, she's not here."

"But her death…"

"I don't know about anyone's death, I don't even understand mine."

"Teaston, you're not dead."

"No, I'm not dead, I'm water."

We remain quiet for a long while. Camila keeps her eyes focused on the line between the sea and the sky. I just watch the sea spray bathing the rocks. In moments like this, words behave like foreign bodies, we reject them, and we need to extract them from our insides. Silence becomes a burden and Camila reaches for my hand. She knows that I will need her help to walk back to the studio; she knows this territory is foreign to me. Camila sets out on the path ahead of me and I follow. But when I turn my head to regard the place of death once more, my eyes catch a glimpse of light, a reflection. I let go of Camila's hand and turn back to where the light came from. Camila keeps walking ahead probably thinking I need distance from her. I find the spot where the reflection came from, and among the rocks, glistening, I see a piece of jewelry. My right hand reaches into a nook between two rocks and pulls out the silver Bedouin necklace that framed the face of the olive woman. The necklace falls into my pocket, my steps become swifter, and I reach Camila who, this time, does not know.

"Are you coming, Teaston?"

"I'm here."

"You seem far away."

"I'm here."

When we reach the studio, I tell Camila I want to spend the rest of the day painting. She stares at me, and for one instant, I believe she can read my mind. No, she cannot read my mind. But her expression, the way in which she looks at me, the pause before uttering her discontent, all of these factors give me the impression that she knows very well what I am thinking. And if she could read my mind, she would know I have a silver Bedouin necklace burning in my pocket. I try to stop my thoughts from forming inside my head. I may fail to contain them there. My thoughts could be broadcast to Camila, to the world. But I do not bow to the whiteness, my thoughts are mine, and nobody knows about them.

"What do you mean, Teaston?"

"I haven't said anything."

"You said you wanted to paint for the rest of the day."

"That's what I thought."

"No, that's what you said."

"Yes, I actually said that. What else did I say?"

"Nothing."

"Nothing, I said nothing."

She pulls me away from the studio and into our bedroom. Camila has a direct way of showing me when she wants to be intimate—she just brings me to bed. I let her take me wherever she wants. In this moment, however, I am more preoccupied with vacating my mind from any thought than with returning her caresses. I do not respond to her, I remain passive, thinking how to stop thinking.

"Teaston, are you here?"

"I'm somewhere."

"No, here, Teaston, here."

Upon hearing those words, I get up from the bed and walk into the bathroom. I sense Camila's burning gaze when I turn my back on her. I close the door. I peel off my clothes and stand naked in front of the mirror. My right hand extracts the necklace from the pocket of my pants; it weighs like death. The necklace glows in the dim light reminding me of her face, her expression before the fall. I grab the two loose ends of the necklace and clasp them together behind my neck. When I look at myself in the mirror I do not find myself. There is only whiteness.

That's all Phillipy can take

This is a day like no other. A broken day. I struggle to keep my thoughts in line, one connecting with the next. The train rolling between the rails. When an errant thought jumps the rails I feel betrayed and I become quiet. Like I am quiet now. Nobody knows when my mind goes astray. Even Camila, she does not know.

I fear Phillipy will show up at the door any minute. I fear him, but I do not know exactly why. Maybe the way he avoids eye contact, or maybe his deviant way of talking. Marcel never told me for how long I need to host Phillipy. I guess for as many days as it takes for people to forget about me. That day may never come; people seem to look for me continuously.

At the door, he is at the door, Phillipy. The thought I just had in my mind was about Camila, her free spirited way to walk around the cliff. Then, this thought of death lands unannounced. Not her death or mine, death as a smell, something in the air, a knock perhaps.

There is no connection.

Phillipy knocks at the door but that does not make a connection. I knew he was coming to knock three times. How could that be a connection?

Phillipy lets himself in as soon as I open the door. He goes to a corner of the studio and starts to unpack his painting paraphernalia. He does not look at me nor does he say hello. I still do not know if I should treat him like a child or like a man, or like something inhuman. I approach him and stand next to him while I observe his agile hands making all sorts of preparations. I feel like slapping him and saying good morning. But I do not.

"Teaston isn't glad to see Phillipy."

"What do you mean?"

"Phillipy doesn't mean anything. Teaston isn't glad to see Phillipy today."

"Are you glad to see me?"

"Phillipy is very glad."

"Glad to see me, or just glad?"

"He hasn't seen Teaston yet."

"Who?"

"Phillipy."

"Phillipy, do you feel death in the air?"

"Death, oh no!"

Dropping brushes and paint tubes on the floor, Phillipy rushes out of the studio and closes the door behind him. Three minutes pass in silence after which he knocks three times. I open the door and let him in again. He has not looked at me yet, not a glance; his eyes focus on the mess spread on the floor. And the thought of mother jumps the rail.

"Phillipy, where's your mother?"

"Mother is on the other side."

"On what side?"

"On the other side from here."

"But, what side is that?"

"The opposite side of life."

"What do you mean?"

"Teaston wants Phillipy to say it but he won't."

Phillipy's face turns desolate. His dodging eyes seem to focus on a place far away or maybe deep inside. His lips start to move forming inaudible words. I know he is hurting. He then sits on the floor, grabs his head with both arms, and starts to rock back and forth, slowly.

"I just want to know about your mother."

"*Maman, maman*."

"Where is she?"

"Phillipy wants to be with her."

"What happened to her?"

"No, Phillipy, don't say it."

"Is she dead? Is that what the problem is?"

"Death, no, no, no!"

Phillipy storms out of the studio again. This time he slams the door shut. I hear him outside mumbling words that I cannot understand. Then I hear when he throws the weight of his body against the door. I think about the sea, the body of the sea, my body sinking. He knocks again, three times.

"Your body, Phillipy, is hard."

"Teaston has to open the door. Phillipy knocked three times."

"Don't lean against the door."

"Three times."

"Where's your body?"

"The body is all around Phillipy."

"Does it feel like water?"

"Like water?"

"Yes."

"Teaston is not making sense."

He knows. He can tell when thoughts are tangled. He may speak in third person but he is linear, he follows one thought with the next. Then I think a bout, no, I think ab out, no, I think about the two men that sat next to me at the restaurant. They were looking at me. Let them look. Who knows what they may find? But Phillipy is right here, outside my door telling me that I make no sense.

"I'm opening the door, Phillipy."

"The door will be opened for the third time."

"I didn't mean to say…"

"Three times, that's all Phillipy can take."

"Are you sure you want to come in?"

He comes into the studio and heads straight to his brushes and paint tubes lying all over the floor. He arranges everything and gets ready to start painting. I watch Phillipy and wonder about his age, his mother, his urge to paint. I wonder about his death, unaccomplished but perhaps approaching.

And my thoughts break apart

and I cannot find the thread

no, not the word, not that word again.

"Death, mine or yours, Phillipy, but death it is."

"Three times, three times, three times, that's all Phillipy can take."

He can smell the lie

At the end of the quay stands this old man who cannot see. His skin has a brown hue, like burnt umber, and his eyes shine like iridescent pewter. He must recognize the spot where he stands by its smell, or maybe he counts the steps from the mimosa tree. I have never asked him how he gets there, but there he is. He talks to everyone who walks by, mainly about things that cannot be seen. As I get close to him he calls my name, "Teaston." If I were not to answer his call, he could not confirm it is me who approaches. There are times when I just turn around and walk away from him. Perhaps he knows it is I, turning away, trying not to be Teaston to a blind old man.

I come close and he turns his face towards me as if he could see me. He smiles. I smile, but not like him.

"What troubles you, Teaston?"

"I don't know."

"Are they still looking for you?"

"Who's looking for me?"

"You know..."

"The *gendarmes*, is that what you mean?"

"The two men."

"A short man and his tall bearded friend?"

"Yes."

"How do you know about them?"

"I hear things."

"I hear things too, but, not everything is real."

"Those two men are real."

"What else have you heard?"

"No, Teaston, don't ask me that."

This is not where I want to be. He cannot see me, yet he sees through me. I start walking away with a soft step while holding my breath.

"Teaston, you don't need to be upset. Please come back."

"I wasn't going anywhere."

"You mean, you were going nowhere."

"I was going nowhere."

"That's what I thought. Where on earth could you go?"

"To the water, maybe."

"Teaston, don't say those things."

"Where are the two men?"

"Haven't they found you yet?"

"I'm not sure."

"Then, they haven't."

"They sat next to me at the restaurant just the other day."

"Yes, I know."

"You know?"

"Yes."

He knows. He listens. He senses my fear. A man, old, blind. I do not doubt him, like I do not doubt death. The serenity of his words lures me. My right hand, the one that grabs on, reaches for his shoulder. I grab on to him. He smiles again.

"Why are the two men looking for me?"

"Teaston, only you know that."

"But you hear things."

"But not everything is real, as you say."

"Are they real?"

"I already told you."

They are real to me, and the old man says they are real to him. But he cannot see them. How would he know? I stand there, next to him, and pretend my mind is at ease.

"Have you ever crossed the Med?"

"No, Teaston, nobody has taken me on that trip."

"There's only water between foreign tongues."

"There's also music, jazz; Thelonious, for example."

"He was dissonant, like my thoughts."

"No he wasn't, he just felt the music."

"I feel death."

"Teaston, how about feeling your music?"

"There's a dissonance."

"You're not really listening. Can you hear the angular melodic twists?"

"That's what death sounds like, I know."

"How do you know that?"

"It's like a leitmotif; it keeps coming back to my mind."

"I don't believe in death, Teaston."

"I hear it, but I don't believe on it either."

The blind old man remains pensive. He can smell the lie.

Most of me

I begin to sink under the clouds, like a sun with no reason, the thin atmosphere swallowing me. If I were to disappear at dusk, I would be content, my body entering the sea in calmness. Myself joining my vastness. This I think when I am alone; among people, I feel persecuted. Prosecuted sometimes. My nature is tumultuous if not confused. Nothing to the day, that is what I am.

Cassis is…

No, not really.

Well.

Cassis is all I fear and all I need. I do not demand death, but I yearn for it. And Cassis is death. I need water, myself as water. And Cassis is water if it is not dirt. I have fallen, my mind has. And Cassis gives me a cliff to fall from. All in one, my life in Cassis blends what I fear with what I need. I am drawn to this place because it gives me everything, because it gives me death, or the possibility of death, at the same time that it gives me water. Cassis offers that.

A swirl of clouds in the red sky warns me that night approaches. I see the dark shape of a stubborn cloud in the horizon, against the red. I stand against death. We should talk to each other, the cloud and I. But the cloud is not aware of me. I have no name tonight. Teaston is not present and cannot be conjured. With no one around, my name is forgotten. Darkness closes in leaving only a sliver of red light in the horizon. There is nothing to fear, for what I fear is when people see me, and at this moment, I am nothing.

Camila joins me as I watch the horizon from the cliff. She touches me. Her touch makes me feel I exist as Teaston, no whiteness, no death wish. She thinks I enjoy the spectacular sunset. I enjoy this bewildering moment but not as peacefully as she might think. For her, the cliff is a viewpoint, a wonderful perspective on the sea below.

"Would you come with me?"

"Where, Teaston?"

"Anywhere, everywhere."

"I'll go with you."

"Even if there's no way back?"

"There's always a way back."

"No, not always."

Camila will not jump with me. Two parallel paths finding their way into the sea. No, she always finds a way back. She wanders every day, traversing hills, crisscrossing the town, but always retracing her steps. She does not think about death like I do. She may have had her death already. For her, the cliff is a sanctuary, a place away from that other place to which she will never return.

"Camila, where do you go when you hurt?"

"I'm not hurting anymore. That's all over."

"Do you ever feel like it could happen again?"

"Not when I'm with you, Teaston, that's why I'm here."

Almost no light left in the horizon. Almost no life left. Camila remains quiet. She could be remembering or she could be forgetting. I look at her face and find that calming expression. Her mind so hermetic, unlike mine, a porous substance ransacked by all. I think she thinks about me.

"Teaston, what happened at the hospital?"

"No, Camila, please."

"Is that what's hurting you?"

"The hospital never existed, there was only whiteness."

"You must remember something."

"No."

"Teaston, where do you go when you hurt?"

"To the sea."

This can be the moment. But she will not come with me. No, she will not. And I cannot force her. Her life is beautiful now, all the misery behind her. She can walk endlessly from dawn till death while hanging her ache from a low cloud.

Another moment passes, my right hand tenses, I begin to dig my nails into the white earth.

From my mouth, "Don't even say it! I won't."

From Camila's mouth, "What, Teaston?"

From my mouth, "There, there."

From someone's mouth, "You're water, you."

From Camila's mouth, "Look at me."

From my mouth, "It's me down there."

From someone's mouth, "Better both."

From Camila's mouth, "Lean against me."

I lean against her while forcing my fingers into the white dirt. I dig hard. I hear a crack and feel the pain as I fracture my middle finger. I hold on to Camila and I hold on to the cliff.

Myself down there.

Most of me.

There, there

I must walk.

I push everything away.

I have to walk.

Everything behind me. Let it accumulate in piles. Nothing from anyone, no. I make a humming noise in the back of my throat that reverberates and drowns the voices. I walk and I hum. One or one hundred kilometers, I do not know. Hum, hum, humming. Nothing else enters my mind.

I feel the wounds falling into the sea. One, the studio, two, the cliff, three, Camila. No, not her. She is not falling. Three, Her Majesty. She needs to fall. And Phillipy? I do not know about him.

A sense of lightness fills me when I walk. I walk more. The road, well, what can the road do? It takes me, it leads me away from the cliff. I go far from that edge, alone.

My face must reveal something because people stare at me when I pass by them. This face is not painted, but I do not tell them that. This must be the face of Teaston.

Go on.

Walk more.

Turning at Rue de L'Arène I confront a massive number of people who seem to be waiting for me.

Oh, no!

I turn around and walk some more, away from the crowds, into a narrow alley that smells of cat piss. A few more turns bring me to the alley behind Marcel's restaurant. The back door is closed. I can knock on this door and tell Marcel that I left everything behind. He will give me that look, with that right eye of his. Maybe he will ask me to sit at my table and have a glass of Bandol.

Don't knock.

I don't.

I turn away, fast and far. And within minutes, I reach a corner where two men talk to each other. Their eyes look down and then up at me, as if conspiring. I go past them and they feign not to care about me. Amateurs. They are incapable of concealing their motives. Let them stay in that corner babbling.

I feel the warmth.

The downcast sun.

And because of it, the sun, I continue walking west, looking for the source of warmth. The cliff is cold, and I am trying to leave it behind me. The whiteness, more than cold. Away, away from all that falls, from all that falls behind.

A tall bearded man steps out of a foyer. He stands in the middle of the road. Ahead of me a shorter man joins him. From a distance, they watch me approach.

Yes, they are…

They are.

I pretend not to recognize them. I continue walking as if I had something urgent to care for. They let me pass them by.

From the mouth surrounded by a beard, "Teaston."

I keep walking away pretending not to hear anything.

From the short man's mouth, "Teaston."

From my mouth, "Teaston isn't my name."

From the mouth surrounded by a beard, "We know what you did."

From the short man's mouth, "Yes, we know."

They say these things as I try to walk faster. The tall one catches up with me on the road and holds me by the shoulder.

From the mouth surrounded by a beard, "Teaston, yes you are."

From the short man's mouth, "Teaston, you."

From my mouth, "I'm not Teaston, I'm water."

The force, the speed, the vehemence of their blows is extraordinary. My head moves from one side to the other. A shoe lodges between my ribs. There is blood. It comes out of my nostrils and from the corner of my mouth. My face feels the coldness of the asphalt. They think I am a murderer.

I am not.

I am nothing.

I lie on the sidewalk. All the surfaces around me are cold, colder than my body. I reach for anything to grab on to. Nothing. I then push up with both of my arms until I stand. Precariously, I stand. The two men have disappeared. I look for them but find no trace. They may be hiding, jumping realms, perhaps. This is not the cliff, but just as deadly.

I retrace my steps and stumble from alley to alley until I reach the back door of Marcel's restaurant. This time I knock as hard as I can. I sit by the door, exhausted, blood dripping from my face. This is how the *garçon* finds me, and alarmed, calls on Marcel. When Marcel arrives, they lift me and drag me inside the kitchen.

"Teaston, who did this?"

"The two men. They're after me."

"What two men?"

"One is tall and has a beard, the other one short."

"But, why?"

"They think I pushed her."

"Who did you push?"

"I just saw her face."

"Teaston, now…"

The *garçon* brings wet towels and starts to clean some of the blood. Marcel's right eye takes flight, inspecting my wounds, looking for a little crack to get into my brain.

"I'll call the *gendarmes*."

"No, Marcel."

"Why not?"

"They will start asking questions again."

"They don't care about that kind of woman."

"But, I do."

Marcel knows not to get involved. He makes sure that I am comfortable and runs out to the bar. He returns with a glass of Bandol and offers it to me.

"Here, this will soothe you."

I rest there for some time, feeling numb, maybe guilty for having walked away from the cliff. There is no point in avoiding the cliff, like there is no point in avoiding nothingness. I hear the interlacing words of the restaurant patrons and the clanking noises in the kitchen. Everything becomes a blur.

"Teaston, look at me."

"There's no way."

"I can make you feel better."

"No, no."

Next to the furnace, Her Majesty stands watching me while drinking from a martini glass. I remain motionless, hurt as I am, but with an urge to flee the kitchen.

"You're my Teaston."

"I'm nothing."

Her Majesty unbuttons her shirt, revealing her large breasts, which she points directly at me. Undisturbed by the comings and goings of the kitchen staff, Her Majesty sways her chest and laughs.

"Teaston, drink from me."

"You're not my mother."

"Here, just a few drops."

"You are not my mother."

"My boy."

"I'm not your boy."

Marcel returns from the bar and kneels next to me. He tries to clean my face with the towels but I push his hand away. The unbearable heat in the kitchen makes me sweat, drips form on my forehead, and when they roll down my face my wounds sting.

"Teaston, what did you say?"

"She isn't my mother."

"Whom are you talking about?"

"No, no... Nobody."

"What really happened to you?"

"I don't know."

"Teaston, please."

"Marcel, what happened to his mother?"

"Whom are you talking about?"

"Phillipy."

"What about Phillipy?"

"He had a mother."

"No, Teaston... Not now. You're hurt. We have to take care of you."

"What happened to her?"

"There, there. Drink some wine."

"Where is she?"

"There, there."

Seems white to me

Camila sits next to me without saying much. She seems absorbed in her thinking, her eyes focusing on a place away from here, maybe that place she would go to if she were not here. She does not need to go anywhere. I fear she does, but she says she came from places she can never visit again. I only know so much, not more. She observes my wounds. Not all of my wounds fell into the sea, rather, many of them remain with me, and some are even visible. Maybe that is what she looks at, my wounds.

She touches me. I lift my eyes and watch her touching me. I watch because I never know what she is really looking at. Sometimes into a void. But, no... she looks at my wounds. There are legion, in my face primarily. The back of her hand moves across my face and I feel her skin in contact with mine. I almost feel her thoughts in contact with mine. But my erratic thoughts jump away even in moments like this. I lose touch with her, with the world. Her hand and my face. My hand and the faces of the fallen. The face of the olive woman, everyman's face, and the faceless of the many I have painted. My faceless self wearing Teaston as a name. The face of the sea, the surface of the sea, rippled.

Camila does not ask what happened to me. I do not expect her to ask, she knows. She does not ignore the wounds; actually, she seems fascinated by them. For a moment, I feel compelled to talk about the two men. How they assaulted me, abruptly as they did, how they identified me at Marcel's restaurant several days ago. But I do not mention them because she may get scared. They still roam the streets, looking for me, or looking for

the fallen woman they left behind just before her life ended. These are dangerous men.

Camila licks one of my wounds. I feel her warm and corrugated tongue covering the field of lost skin. It feels wet. She cares for me in an animal way, detached from human concerns. She goes one by one, licking every cut or abrasion on my face. Is she licking the face of Teaston, or is she licking the face of the hurt, the fallen? I do not ask. Sometimes, like this time, Camila behaves like a loving animal. Her instinctual drive crushes any concept, philosophical or otherwise, that lands on her portal. When she licks my wounds, she must think of me as a hurt kitten. Camila.

"Your face, Teaston."

"Yes."

"Someone tried to change it."

"There's no point in that."

"They tried."

"Yes."

"Do they know you?"

"I don't know myself."

"Teaston, please."

"They only know my face."

"Why did they do this?"

"They think I saw her face."

"Who, Teaston?"

"A face before death, everyone's face."

"The one you are trying to paint?"

"I don't know what I'm trying to paint anymore."

I abandon myself to her caress, this being a furtive moment of peace, a little rock to step on amidst the turbulence. I lie next to Camila and I feel protected. The pain of the blows becomes a memory. And like the rest of my memories, they will disintegrate leaving an invertebrate blur where nothing stands to reason. I rest now, for a moment I can.

"Close your eyes, Teaston."

"I'm afraid."

"I'm here for you."

"I know."

"Close your eyes now."

"Don't leave me."

"No, Teaston, I won't."

I close my eyes and let go of the sights, the sounds, and the uneasiness of the world. I try to remain calm, but soon enough a space opens in my mind's eye.

I tremble.

"Where are you, Teaston?"

"I don't know. Everything seems white to me."

Don't say it

I wait until he knocks at the door three times. He always knocks in the morning at a quarter to ten. I expect him now, even if his presence feels uneasy. Phillipy does not know the way I react to him. Rejection, boredom, embarrassment, these remain a mystery to him. When I open the door he quickly makes his way into the studio. But this morning he makes eye contact for a split second, enough for him to notice the scabs and the bluish tone around my eyes. He resumes his gaze aversion as if bothered. Once again, he turns his face towards mine in the most surreptitious way. And for the first time, I see the green of his eyes and their inquisitive depth. But immediately, without wasting a minute, Phillipy prepares to start painting.

I walk up to him and grab the brush away from his hand, close the acrylic paint tube, and stand between him and the canvas. Phillipy turns his face sideways and stares at the floor. He fidgets. I hear the air flowing hard through his nose.

"Phillipy needs the brush to paint."

"I know."

"Teaston, give the brush back to Phillipy."

"I will, if you wait a moment."

"He can't paint without the brush."

"Phillipy, wait here for me."

As fast as I can, I rush to the bathroom and find the silver Bedouin necklace. I know I hold death, or a token of death, the part of the olive woman that did not sink in the sea, a heavy anchor for such a luminous face. I hold the necklace between my hands and return to the studio where Phillipy still stares at the floor, as if paralyzed. I grab a stool and sit next to the canvas. I don the necklace and look straight at Phillipy.

"Here's the brush. I want you to paint what you see."

"Phillipy sees Teaston."

"No, you don't."

"What happened to Teaston?"

"Paint what you see."

"He can paint Teaston from memory."

"No, Phillipy. Paint what you see in front of you."

And he does. Almost frenetically, Phillipy mixes colors, attacks the canvas with determined gestures, steps back for perspective, smudges the paint with his fingers, spreads fields of colors, and draws lines, all while his tongue hangs out of his mouth in demonic concentration. I feel as if he swallows me, ingesting all of me, and later regurgitating through his brush. I wonder if he knows I will not recognize myself when he finishes. Who would know that? After all, I do not see myself as others do. I do not see myself as anything.

Camila enters the studio and stops to observe Phillipy's gestures. She does not speak to him, she only watches as he renders my deformed image. Her presence means nothing to Phillipy who continues to paint as if he were in a trance. Camila notices the necklace hanging from my neck. She observes it with a perplexed expression but says nothing. She does not court death, not like I do. She then leaves the studio convinced that what I am doing is important to me, that parts of my life are incomprehendible. I feel like yelling, telling her not to leave me, but only silence comes out of my mouth.

Phillipy does not rest for an instant. He paints steadily for three hours. During that time I think about the emptiness, the void inside, the fear that my image will resemble nothing, my sense of fluidity, the cliff, the vastness below the cliff, water, my very substance, Her Majesty taunting me, the years before this year and the life before this life, the whiteness, no, not the whiteness, the faces that fell, the faces that still call me asking to be rendered, my name, not myself, but my name as a representation of myself, the moment when I felt intact, the moments when I felt derailed, the fear of persecution, the harshness of the street on my face, the sense that there is no sense, the kindness of Camila, the darkness of my mornings, the thought that my thoughts make no sense when reality plays tricks on me.

"Teaston, Phillipy painted what he saw."

"Are you sure?"

"He painted what he saw, Teaston."

He painted what he saw.

The tortured face on the canvas reveals my reality, the beating still fresh in my eyes. This is not Teaston; this is a man called Teaston. A portrait depicting a seated man whose facial expression speaks of death. But the lines and the colors seem accurate, sketchy, but accurate, the vacuous expression is real, and the yearning for death cannot be concealed. The necklace shines with an unreal light, as if it had a life of its own. It seems to float over my neck, unwilling to touch the skin of the dead. Phillipy uses a pyramid design to place me simply and calmly in the space of the painting. My folded hands form the front corner of the pyramid. My chest, neck and face glow in the same light that models my hands. The light gives the variety of living surfaces an underlying geometry of spheres and circles. Only my gaze is fixed on the observer and seems to welcome him to this silent communication, a communication foreign to Phillipy for he does not talk to anyone. Behind me, a vast landscape recedes. Winding paths and a distant cabanon give only the slightest indications of human presence. Far away, a vast sea extends into the horizon. On the right corner, a gray promontory links the ground to the sea. My cliff, the last foothold, is bathed by the darkness of the light. Phillipy knows about the cliff. Maybe he has considered it.

"You painted what you saw."

"Phillipy did."

I grab him by his shoulders and force him to look at me. He twists his body like a cat and turns his face away from me.

"Have you ever considered…"

And before saying the word, I remember his rituals, his reactions, and his discomfort around the word. I do not say anything. I let go of him and walk away from the painting.

"Teaston doesn't like to see himself."

"No, Phillipy, that's not the problem."

"Can Teaston see himself in the painting?"

"To see myself, I need to know who I am."

"Yes, Teaston is Teaston."

"How can you be so sure?"

"Phillipy only knows what's there."

"What's really there, Phillipy?"

"Death, a lot of death around Teaston."

He says the word "death" and his whole body contorts. He makes a strong effort to remain quiet, motionless, but his compulsive self has the upper hand. In desperation, Phillipy drops the brushes and paint tubes, and heads for the door in a rush. I hear him slam the door hard on his way out. He knows what he needs to do. His insistence in sameness forces him to repeat things once and again. And as expected, after three minutes, he knocks on my door three times. I do not respond, hoping he will bend his rules by knocking again, or by trying the southern door instead. He does not knock again. When I approach the door, I hear him on the other side breathing heavily, waiting for me to let him in.

"Phillipy."

"Phillipy wants to come in."

"What do you see in the painting?"

"He sees Teaston."

"What else?"

"Phillipy needs to get in the studio to say it. But if he does, he will have to get out again."

"You painted what you saw."

"Yes."

"Then don't say it."

The sea of her skin

A time of confidences.

Not even if I tried.

I long to confide in her, Camila, but I cannot find the truths of my past. She must regard me as an errant soul. This I know because when thoughts force their way into my mind, unannounced, or when they escape my mind, naked for all to see, she touches me as if she was touching an absence. Camila with her smile. Then I try to tell her everything but my words come out slurred, as if from the depths of a cave, from a confused emptiness.

I need to tell her everything; I need her to see inside of me, beyond Teaston, beyond the name that fails to represent me. To hold on, I need her to grasp my depth, if I am to hold on. But my depth lies in darkness many fathoms below my surface—unreachable. The cliff knows about my former days of whiteness, and without effort, it claims me.

Camila claim me, please.

Her touch is obstinate, like my right hand, digging into the safety of the earth. She also whispers, she pushes warm air into my ears, she interlaces her fingers with mine. Not all of me is here, not all of me.

Camila looks over the marks, the wounds. I know she feels the pain and the itch of the scabs. But does she feel the desperation of being nothing? Does she understand the doubts, the drive to yield? I am Teaston to her, I am. I need to be Teaston to myself. I need to confide.

The lights of day arrive with all their intensity, the natural ones, the ones that bounce and jump from surface to surface, livening the pressure points of rooms, the angles of our bodies. The same light returns from her retina whispering to me.

"Camila, I can see you. Can you see me?"

All those lights conjure a sense of existence, a statement of place, a revelation that contains the fears and desires to join that which is hidden. Without light there would be no face. And then.

This is the room, this is the bed in which we lie, Camila and my body. We invent love here and let other people make it. She touches me with the power to touch, with the sobering capacity to dismantle chaos. This is the room where I hide. This is the room where I feel the tide rising. There is her flesh, moist, barely. Mine, wet and oozing salt from the vastness below. I am a creature, a lowly order trapped between the layers of two worlds, or how many worlds.

Fuck you, Teaston! Yes.

My right hand takes her hand.

No, I take her hand and watch how Camila abandons herself to me. She knows my needs. This is how she leads me, this is how she takes over the fear, this is how she inserts herself into me. If you could stay.

Not here, not her. I close my eyes and think of the last place in the world I could run to. Please, not here. A space opens in my mind allowing everything to sip in, like a hideous pore letting the outside in. Her Majesty knows what I am doing, like she knows what I am thinking. Even here, in my bed, Her Majesty mauls me. I turn away from Camila's face and there she is, Her Majesty, naked too, and so white, flaunting her dripping vagina.

Can I disown my mind? Can I live outside of this?

Her Majesty usurps this room like she usurps my mind. The disquieting sight of her vagina invades me. I stand next to the bed, trying to hide my turbulence from Camila.

I consider death.

Naked, I leave the room and run to open the southern door. The day is tired, the lights outside suffocated, and a fragile wind drags over the surface of the earth. There, out there, is the cliff. Not a pretty time for pictures.

I go to it.

"Teaston, Teaston."

That is how they call me. But who calls me now?

The sea, myself, below. The little white caps dance on the surface of my skin. And the keel of a sailboat carves a deep scar across my back. I bleed inside my depth. My depth and my vastness. All the faces in one, all the voices in one. A face, a mouth, swallows me and it cannot be painted. A voice drowns and is never heard off again.

"Teaston."

"I'm not."

"Teaston."

Her voice, Camila's voice, surrounds me. She presses her bare skin against mine and holds me down at the edge of the cliff. I feel the sea of her skin.

Things he cannot see

From the angle where he sits, the blind old man keeps guard over the old port. Nothing escapes him, not a single vibration. He hears every syllable, every cough, the sound of coins falling on the small dish at Marcel's restaurant, the waves crashing against the seawall, the slight hesitation in the speech of liars, the sound of fear. I am convinced he recognizes the sound of death, like an aura, an audible premonition. This draws me to him. He can hear death when all I can do is see its face.

The old man knows when I swallow the last drops of Bandol. He can hear the empty glass as I lay it on the table. He can hear the change in my tone of voice when Marcel gazes at me with that eye of his. When I walk to the end of the quay he smiles, anticipating my failure to veer my course away from him. He senses the fear, my uneasy wish to see death through his eyes.

When I stand close to him, I close my eyes and try to see his world. Nothing happens. When all the colors and thoughts mesh into each other I see only whiteness. That is not his world; his is a rich absence, illuminated by a different light.

My right hand comes to lie on his shoulder. I see how my hand rests there, balancing, barely moving. We do not speak to each other for a while. My eyes absorbing the hues of blue, of myself as water, the ochre over bricks, the green in the flesh of leaves. His skin and the drums of his ears capture everything my eyes cannot see.

"I'd like to see your paintings, Teaston."

"You never asked before. Why now?"

"You never offered."

"But you can't…"

"Yes, I can. I can sense them."

He senses the wounds on my face. He senses my yearning, the fluid that emanates from my mind. But what does he know about me? He could be demented or he could be a farce. Maybe he is a Cyclops with a mind reading eye between his two dead eyes. I fear him, like I fear knowing the horror inside. But once in his presence, I cave, the hollowness of me collapses. Does he have a name? I have a name and what good comes from it, nothing. I am not reducing him to a name.

We walk down the quay without touching each other. I do not need

to lead him, he knows his way with precision. We pass in front of Marcel's restaurant. I notice how the blind old man bows at a pretty lady who touches the rim of her wine glass with her lips. We continue walking and turning until we arrive at the plaza where my Citroën is parked under a purple bougainvillea. He climbs into the car at once. He opens the window allowing the sea breeze to caress him as the car climbs the hill to my studio.

Once we arrive, the blind old man enters my studio and asks to be seated facing the northern light. I offer him a comfortable divan, which he rejects in favor of a stool next to the canvases. He becomes quiet and his old face assumes a sublime expression. He seems to sample the noise of the clock, the buzz of the fluorescent lights, the amalgamated aroma of paint tubes, the vibrating particles of linseed oil, the freshness of turpentine, the murmur of my nervous sweat as it oozes out of my pores.

"Teaston, show me one of your paintings."

I have nothing to show him. I have ruined every canvas, all the lines and shadows covered by fields of white paint. Everyman's face is nowhere. I grab one of the white canvases and place it on the easel right in front of the blind old man. He hears how I position the canvas and how I gasp when I move to the side allowing him full view.

He becomes pensive. And the minutes grow.

"Why, Teaston?"

"Believe me, I've tried."

"Are you afraid of people's faces?"

"No, I'm only afraid of mine."

"What do you see in your face?"

"Whiteness."

The blind old man sits on the edge of the stool and stretches his arm until he reaches the canvas. He moves the palm of his hand over the white field of paint. His touch is soft, empathic even. His fingers trace the edges of the canvas where some of the underlying colors show through.

"Teaston, all the faces are here."

"They're all dead."

"Not all."

"Which one is alive?"

"Your face, Teaston, your face is alive."

"I'm nothing."

"That's not what I see."

The blind old man does not ask to touch any more paintings. He simply gets up and requests to be driven back to the port. I wish for him to stay longer. I need to find out how he knows. But he starts talking about the sea and the mountains, about the glittering mornings and the shadows at dusk, all things he cannot see.

I am...

Why do I want to read this book? I have a wish to know what happens after the first page. Many times, like this time, I open the book and feel a sense of solidarity, as if both, the book and I, were trying to say the same thing. But I never read beyond the first page, so this sense of oneness may be a twisted product of my imagination. And like many times before, I close the book abruptly.

This is a very closed book now.

The book is well bound, the covers are hard, but there is no title, and the pages are not numbered. Is it divided into chapters or sections? Is it written in one language only? I imagine it ends with the words *The End*. No, I will not read the last page; there may be an end there. Is there an end? Whose end?

I place the spine of the book on my left hand keeping the covers pressed together between my thumb and the rest of my fingers. This feels safe; nothing can spill from the pages. Then, I relax the grip enough so that the pages open a little and the air circulates among them. They are all printed in black ink, that much I can tell. There must be a story in these pages, someone's story. I consider fanning the pages and stopping at a random point to read. I grab all the pages with my right hand and bend them slightly like a bow. I fan the pages, but when I try to stop, the thumb in my right hand continues the motion so rapidly that all I manage to see is a blur. The story remains unknown to me. I lay the book down on the table. Whoever wrote the story does not want me to read it.

This is nonsense.

Why would the book be here, in my own house, if I am not supposed to read it? I know I can read the book, like I know I can paint everyman's face, like I know I can forget all about the cliff.

But I do not.

I imagine a book embodying the sea. A book where the pages behave like waves, one flowing into the next. A book as deep as the Mediterranean. A sea of words to immerse oneself into. A book that ebbs and flows expanding and touching the continents. Every ocean, every book. A book that could hold people afloat or swallow them into its bowels, creating life or rendering a suffocating death. A book about death, a little death, or a big death—a final one.

I think I have died a few times, none of them final. There is that sense of moving from one's life to another with an intermittent space where death comes to visit. When I left the whiteness, death surrounded me. That was not a final death, although it felt hard and devastating. Those are the times when death comes uninvited, a result of miserable experiences. But a good book cannot tell the story of a miserable time where death comes as a consequence. That is an easy death. This book, the one I cannot read, the one whose title eludes me, must tell the story of a death resulting from a need to die, not as an expected result, but a death that comes because it has to.

But I have not read the book. It remains a mystery to me in its closed and unnumbered pages. The book could also be a lie, apocryphal even. It could tell the story of another time and other people unrelated to me. The thought that the book may tell a story relevant to me is pedestrian and basic. Why would this book bother with my ordinary life? After all, I am nothing, nothing to the sidewalk, or to the paper and glue that make this book. But the author must be in the book, the author is the book, even if the book does not succeed in being the whole author.

Like this book, I have no name. People call me *Teaston*, as people call this book, *book*. And that is what I fear most, the fact that people talk to me as if I were Teaston. They address me with a conviction I cannot share. How can anyone know who I am if they cannot read me? Like this book, the text of my life is confused. Camila seems to know more about me than anyone. Maybe she reads about me during those long morning walks. No, that is impossible because she still calls me by my name. If she knew all about me, something that I cannot even do myself, she would treat me as if I were water.

I wish I could find myself in this book, in the unread passages and the white spaces between them. If I could only read beyond the first page.

The author is the book.

The book has no name.

I do not have a name.

I am…

My mind with me

I walk into the wolf's mouth.

They need to know, the *gendarmes*, and I need to find out. Three of them, dressed in blue, sit around a table drinking something, coffee maybe, or pastis. I recognize one of them because he went to my studio to ask questions. The other two are new faces to me. They watch me as I enter their world, unannounced and abruptly. I say nothing; I just look at them and try to imprint their faces in my memory.

They talk among themselves while glancing at me sideways. They drink some more, pretending I am not in their realm. I stand quietly looking at them until the face I know stands and approaches me.

"*Monsieur...?*"

"Teaston."

"Yes, of course, Teaston."

"I was assaulted."

"You were?"

"Yes, I was."

"Are you here to tell us about it?"

"No, I am here to ask questions."

"But that's what we do."

"I know."

The two new faces put down their drinks and come to join their colleague. They look at me as if they were looking at a circus rat, intrigued and repulsed at the same time.

"You took a few blows in your face. I can see that."

"There were two men, one is short and the other one tall with a beard. Have you seen them?"

"*Monsieur* Teaston, why would anyone want to hurt you?"

"That's exactly what I want to ask you."

"If you don't know, who else will know?"

"That's not the question. Have you seen those two men?"

"No, *Monsieur* Teaston, we have not seen anyone like that."

One of the *gendarmes* takes a form and starts to fill it out. He then hands me the form and asks me to fill the rest. I do not write anything and return the blank form back to him. He raises an eyebrow and blows air through his nose.

"Has the pride of France discovered anything about the woman who jumped from the cliff?"

"The one you saw?"

"I didn't see her, I saw her face."

"Yes, you told me that."

"What do you know about her?"

"We don't know much. A streetwalker, perhaps. No one has come looking for her."

"Nobody."

"No."

"How about those two men, have they asked about her?"

"*Monsieur* Teaston, I don't know who you're talking about."

"Even the blind old man saw them. A short man and his tall friend with the beard."

"A blind man saw them."

"Yes."

Gendarmes, imbeciles, rigid marionettes. I look at them trying to find an opening, an angle that would allow reasoning to enter their brains. Three uniformed bodies, oozing blue, return a wooden look at me. I avoid their stare and look around the dirty station, at the clock, at the file cabinets, at the pictures of disappeared children on the wall, at the worn-out chairs in the waiting area. And there, sitting placidly with a cigarette dangling from her red lips, is Her Majesty. I immediately turn away from her but she still catches my eyes.

From Her Majesty's mouth, "What hit you in the face, Teaston?"

From my mouth, "No, no."

From the *gendarme's* mouth, "So, the blind man didn't see them."

From my mouth, "Yes, he did."

From Her Majesty's mouth, "Oh, Teaston look at me."

From my mouth, "No way."

From the *gendarme's* mouth, "*Monsieur* Teaston, do you mean to say yes or no?"

From my mouth, "Yes, but no."

From Her Majesty's mouth, "I've something for you."

From the *gendarme's* mouth, "The blind man cannot see."

From my mouth, "No, he cannot... but yes, he can see them... but no, I'm not looking."

From Her Majesty's mouth, "Here, you have it."

Her Majesty sticks the cigarette between her open legs. After making strange movements with her pelvis, she takes the cigarette and puts it back in her upper lips. A column of smoke rises between her legs.

The ochre of the station, the blue of their uniforms, and the red of her lips merge into each other giving birth to whiteness. I feel thwarted and impossible. To the door I run dragging my mind with me.

Into the sea I swim

They know I saw her, the two men, and they want her back. I do not keep her away, death does, or the sea.

First Bandol.

Marcel is quiet with me; no words come from him, only hasty glances that may have a meaning. But I rest, repose, relax, at my table, keeping a low level of awareness, watching the people that come to the restaurant to occupy tables and spend time and money. I look at them; I do not want to be them. I am satisfied with being something I do not understand. But I am not satisfied with being a person called Teaston.

I need to know more, about myself, about Camila. What do I really know? Very little. I may have lived a whole life, but I am not sure for how long I have being Teaston. And there is no one to ask. No, there is no one. I have no way to learn more about myself. And worst of all, my mind plays tricks on me. I do not trust my mind. But there is no other mind to ask.

Second Bandol.

Marcel stands in front of me and makes gestures with his hands. Covertly, he points at two men that sit at a table across the restaurant. There, this time far away from me, the short man and his tall bearded friend take residence. Where are the *gendarmes*?

The air goes into my lungs in a long, slow, rhythm. My face, I keep turned away from them, regarding how the sea lifts the bottom of the boats and licks the seawall. Another breath and I lift my glass and finish the wine in one long gulp.

Marcel goes over to the two men and asks what they want. Blood, maybe. He then comes around my table on the way to the bar. His right eye is bursting, the arteries crisscrossing the sclera, a protuberant desperate globe.

"They asked about you."

"What?"

"They asked for your name."

"Did you…?"

"No."

"What else?"

"They want to drink Bandol."

"Why Bandol?"

"I don't know."

Marcel rushes back to the bar and leaves me alone at my table. I do not look in their direction; I continue to admire the sea.

My name, they want to know my name. Disoriented men, confused men. What good a vacuous name does? They will not find me by calling me. Teaston, who cares what that sounds like, it does not conjure me, it represents none of me. Like a snake, I slip out of my name. I even drown my name.

From the bar, Marcel's right eye scans the restaurant. I wave at him. He seems tremulous, and without paying attention to me, he returns to the table where the two men sit and brings them two glasses of Bandol. After serving them, Marcel turns away and stops at another table where he listens to a young woman. His right eye, however, jumps and swivels in all directions. He then comes to my table and I notice drops of sweat forming on his forehead.

"They asked for your name."

"Marcel, I don't have a name."

"Teaston…"

"Wine, just bring me wine."

Third Bandol.

I know they are looking at me. They are even drinking my wine. They come here to find her through me. They want to find her, but they do not know I have no possession of her. She jumped. I did not. I did not join with her. I did not hold her, or touch her. I only saw her face.

- a shimmering skin. Light falls all over, the sun that is. Pricking the first layer of water, the sun, getting under it and making it shine. An extensive skin, vast even. I know I can break that skin. I can go through it and make my way deep. Once, I anchored myself below the harbor, throwing the line up to the surface to hang there. I know that will make me feel safe.

A white cap on the surface of the sea, blame the wind. Then another. They quickly procreate, making more of themselves with the wind as their father. I try to count the waves while avoiding looking at the two men. I know where they are. I do not need to look at them to avoid looking at myself. They know she left them. She left me too. But I do not contain her; I cannot even contain her image, her face. She left all of us. The white caps know, they applauded her fall.

I stand and move away from my table leaving behind the empty glass. The wine is inside my body; it reaches all my shores. The two men follow my moves, I know they do, but I pay no attention to them. I look at the sky instead, a layer of purple on top, a thin layer of intense red and yellow in the middle, and a layer of deep blue underneath. Across from the restaurant, through the thick layer of tourists, the seawall awaits me. The edge. The dividing element between myself as Teaston and myself as water. Away from all, the mind that binds me, the fear of an enveloping whiteness, my hand, the right one, the layers of paint, white paint, the faces, the men that persecute me, myself following myself, I walk to the seawall. At the seawall, I shed my shoes, my shirt, and my name. I sink my head first through the surface of the sea. Then, my body enters my body. And I swim, into the sea I swim.

Why your presence?

You have a strange presence, Camila. I only exist here; I even attempt to paint here.

You, you walk.

I know you discover truths when you walk. There is even death, sometimes only a little death, like Lucio. You don't know him well, the cherub, he could be your son, but he is not. He sacrificed himself.

The little death.

You come from before, you walked before, and you walked next to me that very first time. I go astray, and you walk next to me. That is who you are, Camila. You are something beyond me. I like to think of you as the earth, a moist certainty under my feet, an extensive realm at the edge of my body, my body as water. When I swim in the ocean, when I dive deep letting the air out and the water in, when I feel like not breathing anymore, you grow under me. I could see myself dying, but you reject the idea.

Camila, I wish I could paint you. I wish I could render your face, your eyes, after a long walk. But you are boiling with life, you are wanting from here. The faces, the ones that haunt me, are all dead; their wants are from somewhere else. Your face floats, detached.

You walked with me, up the hill, when I had not dreamt of you. I did not call you; you simply knew that I needed you. Coming from where you came, Paradise maybe, a world I imagine grander than this with castles and riches, and very long afternoons, you chose to grab my hand.

I,

with nothing to offer, a nameless man, can only wonder.

Why, Camila?

Why your presence?

Wait for my arrival

This is my boat.

This is my boat floating over water.

This is my boat floating over myself, gliding over my skin, its hull a membrane separating my two bodies.

I can float, over myself I can. I go far away from the shore watching the lights die away in the distance. A massive amount of earth leaning against my body, the mountains, the cliff, a jagged edge, rocks, pricking my flank. I foam over, I blow a thin layer of myself into the air.

The wind knows my name. It does not call me "Teaston;" it calls me "whoosh." That is my name when I sail away from the shore. I know it because my body reacts with ripples, a wave sometimes. In the summer, when the wind dies, I cannot get far away into myself, and my name dies as well. I feel more vulnerable then.

My boat undulates over my back scratching my skin. I steer it close to the wind, gaining speed and distance, while carving long elliptical scars. My boat gliding over my body, my breathing separate from my being.

I fall into myself and, for the moment, I am submerged.

I do not need gills to breathe underwater. What do I need them for? I am within myself, living inside my own body. I hold my breath until the two bodies of water fuse, and then I open my mouth wide to allow the true exchange, water into water. This is not how I die; this is how I live. Swimming through my silent self, breathing with a soundless lung.

People call my name luring me into their world. I do not answer. Here I exist without fear, away from those who try to find me. Her Majesty does not dare, not deep into the sea. And the two men that persecute me would not be able to breathe underwater. My vast kingdom lies in front of them, embracing the seawall, rounding the cliff, all of me right in front of their eyes, with my white crests and my moods. And when they try to hold me, I slip through their fingers, wet and cold.

I know those faces are here, around me. They resist living on the surface where others can see them and ask for their motives. They joined the sea because they had no other choice. Even Lucio, the cherub, he did not fall. And the olive woman, she looked at me in the last instant to tell me. Their faces are washed of past concerns. Now they show themselves as elongated greens or purples, like Greco apostles.

Underwater, the faces swirl around me, Lucio and the woman, and everyman who made the same choice. Like a school of submerged ghosts they swim together whispering my name: "Whoosh." And I hear no other sound. I belong here, deep under the sea, and these faces share my space. And if I raise them to the surface, or attempt to render them as ex-living people on my canvas, the white foam is quick to reclaim them. That is why all my canvases turn white—the frothy sea swallows them.

All the faces the face. Like a mind that knows me, Camila is transparent. Sometimes I reach with my hands trying to touch her.

Camila.

And I touch nothing.

The long morning walks take her face away from me, her voice too, and then I shiver, fearing the others will come in to fill the void. Camila's face does not swim inside my body; she only exists on the surface. Transparent, over my cliff.

When I.

When I grab on to her.

When I grab on to Camila, I feel dry, elevated over waves and rocks, the urge to dislocate myself making a landing on her. Where she came from, losing yourself is a lie, an unacceptable lie. That is why she will not join me in the deep.

I see blue and green, light from above, no reds. Like in midair, I float on a wet sky, with another wavering sky above. My cells disintegrate, swelling, yielding away their oxygen. And the faces miss their former oxygenated redness that makes them people. I paint those faces, elongated, deformed and hermetic. I try to reclaim them. But the lines and colors become confused, and the whiteness stretches over them.

I open my mouth to sing, and water, my body as water, fills me. And as I yield, to join myself, my right hand thrashes violently. It grabs the anchoring line, bleeds when the edge of a barnacle splits it apart, pulls. The boat yowling, ribs against ribs, pulled from below while wanting to sail away alone, unencumbered by my body. My right hand, the one that paints, the one that writes, no, no, the one that grounds me to the cliff, to the life I know, pulls hard on the anchor line, it catapults me over the gunwale. So much air now, salty, so much air.

The sun knows to dry me. The wind knows to usher me into the old port. The voices know to wait for my arrival.

A spineless creature that needs to die

I am naked.

Camila loves to see me this way.

A lot of skin surrounds me. A layer of epidermis, breathing. If I were to sink, in my own water, my volume would come to the surface. Camila, look at my shell, the leathery yellow that separates my inner fluids from my extended fluids. I revel in the feeling, a feeling that scares me.

Once again, Camila takes my penis and swallows it. All gone! I have a penis, composed of spongy tissue, blood vessels, skin, and who knows what else. She takes it all and makes it disappear. Camila, where…? I do not want to lose my body, my penis, my mouth, myself. I need to stay here on the surface. Yes, she likes to touch everything that comes to the surface, the dry part of me, the earthy Teaston.

She moves her hands over my body, beginning with my head, my neck, my chest, my crotch, and ending with my feet. I am present. I am dry. I try to do the same with her. To touch her. But my hands puncture the air and grab nothing. Come Camila, come... My right hand traces the space where I think Camila stands. My right hand gathers an empty pale air.

Camila rushes to grab me before I become totally limp. She works my penis until I become larger than myself. I cannot see her hands or her mouth, but somehow the miracle happens. I am in this world, the world of the aroused. She does not say a word, but I believe she is the one touching me and making me think I exist as an animal.

I am not Teaston. But I am something other than Teaston. Can I be an animal? I am an animal, look at my penis. I am a beast. I exist as an extension of my crotch. An animal that lives and dies according to my level of arousal. When the water claims me, I feel aroused, a serpent of the sea, a splendid monster. When the earth grounds me, I feel limp, a spineless creature that needs to die.

I wish I could laugh

With its white body and black wing tips, the seagull seems as certain of itself as any bird. Flying over me and coming near to tease me. I run trying to dodge it, and with every step, I come closer to the cliff. Ample space for the seagull to fly. Around me, as I sit on top of the promontory, the space grows, and the seagull relishes.

The seagull laughs.

Making long passes over me, up into the sky, down as close to the cliff as it can, the seagull mocks me. Laughing, laughing, beating its wings, and laughing. I sit watching the mockery, unhappy, my right hand pocking the ground in search of a hold.

I can hear it, the laughter.

It flies in frenzy, from the sky to the sea, to the sky, to the sea. A mistaken seagull. At one point it punctures the sea, and then it punctures the sky, looking for fish up above the cliff. It seems to blend the two blues, feeling comfortable in both. I yearn for both, but I cannot fly.

This bird flies in the night as if it were morning, confusing the stars with the morning dew. My right hand finds a place to dig itself deep. Now I know I am safe. The bird laughs and ridicules me, in its day or night routine, in any of its blues.

I lean back and watch the seagull fly.

It soars.

The black wing tips spanning the earth high above me. I cannot recognize its face, a beak like any other, and the black eyes, no wrinkles to speak of, no grimaces. But the laugh, a brilliant mockery of my name.

"Teaston, Teaston."

"I cannot join you."

"Teaston."

"I cannot fly up into the sky."

Confused, the seagull flies into the heat wanting to fly into the snow. And the air burns in its heat when it sees me arrive. We boil in the heat. The bird beats its wings in desperation, high up into the sea. I wish I could. But, no… I can only fly into the bottom of the sky.

I call out to the seagull. As if the creature would care for me. I still call out. It laughs at me. Making figures in the sky, it laughs. With tremendous speed it throws itself into the sky below. I feel it in my chest, the white plumage parting my own body, digging with its beak into my flesh. It rummages through me until it snatches a silver fish. With its prey secure, the bird ascends up into the sea in a brilliant flight. This bird is confused; it thinks my heart is its home.

Easy, easy.

No point in desperation.

Madness has its own rhythm.

So I breathe, my right hand still holding the ground keeping me from trying. The Gaul of the Sea knows the confines of my spirit. It plays its seductive game in front of me, teasing me. I know I cannot emulate it, a lesser creature I am. I know this bird may have seen the faces of the fallen. Flying with them, accompanying them on their last journey. Maybe even laughing at them. Stupid bird.

"Teaston."

"I knew it."

"Teaston, Teaston."

"No! Fucking bird."

As night falls, I consider sleeping right here at the cliff. My right hand grounds me. I am safe. I wonder if I will confuse the morning dew with the stars. I wonder what my body looks like at dawn, when nobody has yet carved through me. Heaviness presses on me. The air flattens me against the ground. I look into the sky, at the sea, wanting to find the white and black plumage of the taunting bird. There is no bird. There is no laugh. I imagine the creature sleeping at the seashore, dodging the surf in its sleep. I wish I could join it. I wish I could laugh.

The white foam dances

One...

Two...

Three knocks at the door and when I open, Phillipy enters my studio sweating profusely and mumbling robotic words. He passes by me, ignoring my greeting, and quickly prepares to paint something that must be boiling inside his head. In his rushed movements, Phillipy steps on a tube of deep-cadmium red sending the warmth of the color all over the floor.

"Oh, Phillipy screws up. He's a screw-up."

"Won't you say good morning?"

"Can't do it, Phillipy is very busy."

At once he starts to paint. With large brushes he gestures widely, sweeping from side to side on a fresh canvas, spurting paint everywhere. He then takes thin brushes and besieges smaller areas with speed and precision. The sweat covers his face and damps his shirt. I hear deep breaths in and out of his nose, like a tortured bull.

I never know what Phillipy thinks. I try to guess but he seems entrenched in a form of concreteness that defies explanation. His presence creates an uneasy feeling, a sense that life is concave and we are distorted images of ourselves. Camila manages him better than I do. When I leave they talk to each other, I think. I wonder what stories they tell.

"Come back."

"Phillipy, I'm here."

"No, not Teaston, she."

"Who?"

"*Maman*. Come back, *Maman*."

The colors are now merging into each other. A few lines suggest a face, the face of a woman, but they become completely distorted by other lines and fields of blue.

A vein pulsates on Phillipy's forehead.

He starts to lash at the canvas and to throw paint at random covering whatever figure is there. Phillipy then covers his ears with his hands and starts to howl loudly while rocking his body back and forth. The sound is raw, a visceral hurt, an inconsolable yearning. And quickly, with both hands, he lifts the canvas over his head and smashes it against the easel breaking the entire ensemble apart.

And like a wounded beast, an angry beast, he howls, he howls.

I walk around him pushing away broken pieces of wood and paint tubes. I am tempted to lay my hands on him and try to soothe him. But I fear him. I do not know the cause of his misery and I doubt he will tell me. I step back and watch as Phillipy continues to rock. His howling echoes inside the studio, inside my brain. He does not look at me at all, but I know he is aware I am right here, next to him.

"Phillipy, Phillipy."

I get no answer, no recognition.

"Phillipy."

His eyes open, two burning hells staring at me enraged. He looks at me but he does not see me. And at once, he grabs my right arm and digs his ten fingers deep into skin and muscle, pressing against my bones, pulling all my nerves. His hands crush me. I feel the pain. The air keeps coming out of his nose, fast, faster.

"Does Teaston know where she is?"

"No, I don't know anything."

"Why not?"

"I don't know."

"He doesn't know, Teaston doesn't know."

"No, I don't know."

Phillipy lets go of my arm. He screams *"Maman"* at the top of his lungs and bites his lower lip. Blood starts to drip like paint. He then falls to the floor and starts to rock again, slowly this time. The man/child whimpers as if a deep hurt wants to exit his body. I simply watch him in silence; he seems to have forgotten about me.

Camila, where are you? Just when I need you, you walk away. Come and talk to him, you know how to do that. What to say? What to say to a distressed child who behaves like a man who behaves like a child? Can he feel that I am here? Do I exist outside of him? Or even, how do I exist for him, in what form, in what context? I am not part of his world, that world that consumes him where nobody can enter. That world is shattered, I can tell.

After a while, Phillipy calms down and stops rocking. His broken lip quivers but forms no words. He simply lies on the floor surrounded by paint, blood, scattered pieces of wood and a torn canvas. I know the man/child is alone; we are not different in that sense. I am also surrounded by the pieces of my broken life.

I help Phillipy get on his feet. I hug him hard, hard. He leans on my shoulder with his face turned away from mine. This is the closest we have ever been. I can feel his weight, the corpulence of a man, and the trembling yearning of a child. And as I hug his tense body, I can feel myself in him. I then turn his head and look at him directly into his eyes. I press my face against his face and feel the coolness of his sweat against my skin.

"Let's go out, Phillipy."

"Where's Teaston going?"

"Let's go to look at the sea. It's calmer there."

"But Phillipy needs to paint her."

"You can paint her there."

Phillipy gathers his brushes and paint tubes and prepares to follow me out of the studio. On the way out, I grab one of my canvases with a thousand layers of faces under white paint. This is all he needs; the rest is deep inside his mind. We walk towards the cliff. I lead the way and Phillipy follows. The cliff does not move; it rests there like an immobile giant. I can see its contours, the loose rocks and the patches of grass. And as we get near, the cliff kneels down to open the view for us. The vast sea below, my body there.

"Phillipy can paint here."

"I know you can."

And he does. Phillipy starts to mark the canvas I brought for him. Stroke after stroke, I see him go deeper into his world. Deeper, deeper. For a second he lifts his eyes to look at the sea as if he were looking at his mother.

Deeper.

When the waves crash against the rocks the white foam dances. I like to see those figurines, the children of my body. I like to see them dance. Could that be my world? Full of white children and a body that reaches far, curving at the end, and finally falling off.

I like to see them fall. No, I like to see them dance.

A face emerges from the canvas, faint, unrecognizable, a woman of sorts, maybe an angel. Phillipy seems to paint her from memories deep inside his brain. For every clear line he makes, another stroke, a deep memory, blurs the edges. There is a smile, now it is gone. An eye opens up, cries, and then it closes. The light around her image turning into shadows. Every stroke unleashing a continuous transmigration.

"*Maman*, stay."

"What, Phillipy?"

"Can Teaston make her stay?"

"I don't know."

"Phillipy is going to her."

"No, no, don't…"

"*Maman*."

When his body crashes against the rocks the white foam dances.

IIII

The children I never had

Do not jump tracks.

You, thoughts of mine, disjointed.

Please stay connected.

He is not. I know he is not.

He is not my son but like a son who imitates, he paints with passion
the people that matter most to him like his *maman, ma man, a man, man, an*

or as he says the woman that lies on the other side of here, a place

death as a place

D-E-A-T-H

that word he could not pronounce because the sentiment makes his
mind twirl

my mind twirls

where is it going?

and forces him to enter a world where the count of three ascends to
a higher order forcing him to repeat, repeat, repeat, as if the very action
would dissipate the anxiety of being a different child or man

a man, child, a dwarf man, a giant child

but different from everyone he has ever encountered in spite of the
protection Marcel tries to provide for him

as he protects me from the *gendarmes* and the mayor himself who looks
for me, no, no

all looking for explanations I cannot offer in the same way that I
cannot explain that Phillipy just wanted to join his *aman, man* or *manan*
like any other child or man who makes no sense

I make no sense. Where is the sense?

of his existence, Phillipy, because he is different from everyone who
knows how to talk to other people or look at them in their eyes or even
understand that there may be a person inside those bodies with feelings
and minds of their own separate from his mind, the theory of mind, others

or my mind, whose mind?

his mind which cannot comprehend the concept of otherness

oh! there, ness, other, ness

a concept that escapes him like so many other concepts he missed

in his short life as the son

he is not my son

of a bartender who ignores the severity of his child's condition and only wants him to learn how to paint

how to die

no, he already knew

how to die

as if painting would give him the life he does not have or the sense of universal cohesion when the man who teaches him how to paint is as confused about his own self

the self, as if we knew where to find it

you bastard!

confused as the poor student who tries to find an answer when the possibility of finding such an answer fleets from me and from poor Phillipy, Phillipy

he expected me to help him hold on to the image of his *shaman*, no, *maman*, when I cannot even hold on to the image of myself or the name that people use to call me

Teaston, Teaston, Teaston, Teas…

because everything seems oblique or distorted at best

without the hope

of ever

finding anything solid about me in this life that seems more fluid than ever before, where my body demands to join the vast body of water in front of this town called Cassis

with its boats and shore

and the rocks that hug the high cliffs from where the sea looks magnificent and from where people lose touch with the ground forever to die

d-e-a-t-h again

so many deaths

leaving only the fleeting image of their faces which I try to render in vain with my pathetic brushes knowing that what I try to do is impossible because people cannot be brought back to life

or even remembered

as they are in that last instant before they leap into their true selves

the place where they all hope to be but barely dare to explore

dark rooms of the mind

you motherfucker mindless mind!

at a time when nothing else seems valid or when they do not have a hand like my right hand

this hand

that insists in holding on to the ground for some unknown reason that still escapes me

like my past or the time of whiteness, whiteness

I hate to remember

everything around me turns a little white

the little bastard

my grasp on reality weakens

do not leave me, you mind

like my grip on Camila who wanders, wanders, around

and seems to fade away from me when I need her most but happens to be there when I need her most

a contradiction

that confuses me and makes me lose my exposure, composure…

as much as when Her Majesty decides to show her face and who knows what else in the worst moment with no regard for the integrity, interiority, intricacy of my mind

inviting me to join her in lewd activities

lewd

that I detest

as if I were a puppet or a toy when she very well knows that our time together is over that I only wanted her when everything around me was white

the bastard

not the case now

although I am starting to have doubts because I feel persecuted, prosecuted, per se, by real people who seem to dodge other real people

I saw them, they hurt me, really, for real

who is to tell where that will lead unless

I

decide to join my body and turn into water once and for all and hold the faces of the fallen in my arms as the children I never had.

Tell me, Teaston

The cliff falls behind me. No, it does not. I walk away from it and towards my studio. As I turn around I see the cliff standing there. It was there before me, it will go nowhere now. Under my arm, the canvas Phillipy left behind drags me down. I should have... No, why kill her again. She is already dead. When I enter my studio, I find Camila cleaning the mess Phillipy left behind. She looks at me.

"Teaston."

"No, no."

"What happened?"

"I don't really know."

"There's paint everywhere."

"There's death everywhere."

Without looking at her, I go into the bedroom and sit on the bed covering my head with a blanket. I rock back and forth, like Phillipy did, not uttering any sound, not wanting to know about colors or faces. Camila follows me and sits next to me. She seems to know. How does she know what I think? How can she tell what my fears are? It feels like my thoughts are broadcast, like she can hear the tumult inside my head.

"He jumped."

"No, Camila, please don't."

"And his mother?"

"He painted her."

"Is she dead?"

"She's dead already."

"Teaston."

"He wanted her."

"You didn't…?"

"No, I just wanted him to paint."

"He's in the sea."

"Yes, but he's not my son."

The afternoon goes long and my thoughts go haywire. Camila stops asking questions and seems to leave again. Like a wandering spirit she roams through the hills, a lonesome self, without me. The sweat is dry now and the blanket feels heavy. I stop rocking and contemplate going down to the port to speak with Marcel, and maybe the *gendarmes*. But if I do? No, no, I have to do it.

When I go back into my studio I take the painting Phillipy made at the cliff and hide it between two of my blank canvases. His last gesture, I need to save it. I then head out the studio and into my Citroën. As I roll down the hill, I hear a soft hissing sound coming from the back seat.

"Teasssssssssston."

"Oh, no."

"Teaston, honey, here's to you."

On the rearview mirror I see Her Majesty lifting a glass of champagne and toasting.

"I'm not looking."

"Yes you're."

She drinks half of the glass and starts to undue the buttons of her blouse. She sheds her blouse and throws it in the front seat. A red blouse. She then proceeds to take off her brassier. The mirror shows her breasts hanging loose, bobbing up and down as the Citroën approaches the old port.

"Teaston, touch me."

"I'm not touching anything."

"Grab them."

I stop the car in the middle of Rue de L'Arène and run away from it. I do not look back. I die to get away from all the people that invade me, that follow me, that want to make me part of their lives, or their deaths, when I cannot even define my own life or death. I run. The smell of cat piss again. I run.

At Marcel's restaurant, my table is empty. I am not at my table, not yet. But as soon as I occupy it, the gravity of the day descends on me. He fell, I saw him fall. He became part of my body. No, he became a figurine in white foam. No, he died. No, he became my child. No, foam, only white foam. I do not know. Yes, I know, I was there just this morning.

Marcel sees me arrive and prepares the glass of Bandol. After he takes care of a few customers, he brings the glass to me and lays it on the table with his typical flair. I wonder if he can also read my mind. Can he tell what I am thinking? Does he know that Phillipy was with me when he painted death, and then died? Maybe that is why Phillipy feared the word "death." Does Marcel know that? Can he tell by looking at me? I take the glass of Bandol and drink it at once. Marcel notices the impulsive gesture. He serves another glass and brings it to me.

"Tell me, Teaston."

Even if you do not listen

Only when and even when all the walls had the same color

a white color

unlike the sea that surrounds me now

a white color that held my thoughts

in place

keeping them from spilling all over, from seeping into other people's minds

so common now and dangerous

yes, dangerous

because Marcel must know without me saying a single word about his son

not my son

who no longer paints and lives in water or in my body but not being my son his veins cannot take in the salt and he is bound to float to the surface and burst when the sun heat hits him

heat hits, hard

and the fluids in his cavities boil like a fever spreading all over his disfigurement, his broken skull and fractured spine, turning him into a fish or a creature that lived in a world of his own that nobody ever understood

including myself

I cannot reach the place he held as his own, the world he inhabited in solitude trying to free himself from the impulses that brought him to my door

knocking, knocking, knocking

wanting to paint because he could and wanting to bring to life those that left like his *maman* or even my own self when I knew that the self he painted was already dead

nonexistent

but I insisted on him painting it anyway as if it would redeem who I am not

I reject that image

but he was capable of feeling and bringing to live the very absence of his fears the ultimate corroboration that his *maman* is on the other side in the place he cannot mention

with his lips

although his mind possibly speaks the word over and over

death, death, death

as if the locution will make it more real than it already is

a presence that I feel continuously around me

death, death, death

compelling me to view the sea, my body, from the edge of that cliff that holds my last footing in this concrete world that I would have already left if my right hand was not so self-ruling and obstinate to dig into the ground even when I resist to hold on to

I know not to

I do know not

I do not know

the reason

strong enough to keep me here contemplating how my mind plays tricks on me in front of all these people who may want to hurt me or at least drown me without me finishing the portraits I must finish as a painter or as a man who needs to reconcile all the deaths into one face for all to see

I fear

another question or doubt as to what is real around me when I do not know what is real for others or if others are real to begin with

or to end with

which is more important to me

for the end the end the end

seems to loom over like a bad cloud or like a storm over the Mediterranean, that formidable name ancient and blasphemous that represents my extended body the one I have not dared to join but that waves at me continuously with its white crests making fun of my prostrated, prostate, pro state, will

my fragmented will

the splitting of the real and unreal that carves through my brain and makes me think of the time when everything was white

a time

that starts to resemble a lot my current moment, this moment that weighs on me with its deaths and its persecutors and the doubts about myself and about my name and about who I was before the whiteness before I came to this town at the edge of a cliff that claims me with the strength of an ancient life or at least a fluid life that wants me back as if I belonged

forever denying me the chance to be something other than Teaston

Teasssssston

no, not again

I live afraid that I may not reach that moment of veracity where the faces that I see and the voices that I hear are as real as my painted image

come, all of you

come and ask me to tell you

I will tell you

I will tell you what dwells inside my mind

to you

I

will, even if you do not listen.

Teaston, Teaston, Teaston

He sits in the same place, as if in a throne, surrounded by the ebb and flow of fears and desires, the blind old man. All the loose words flock to him and he picks them out of the air. That is how he commands the quay. I never see anyone talking to him, at least not the way I do. He knows when I approach him, somehow he knows. And once he centers on my presence, all I can do is confess.

"Was it difficult, Teaston?"

"To tell what I saw?"

"Yes, what else?"

"I don't know anymore."

"Was Phillipy looking for her?"

"His *maman*?"

"Who else, Teaston?"

"He will never find her."

"No, not here, maybe in the sea."

"Yes, we all seem to end there."

"Did you explain to Marcel?"

"I'm not sure, I told him something, but I don't know what that was."

"Teaston?"

"My thoughts, my thoughts just don't…"

The blind old man turns his face away from me. I want to hold him, make him look at me with his hollow eyes. But I fear touching him, I fear he may say things I am not ready to hear. So I start to move away from him in silence, taking cat steps, joining with the multitude that walks down the quay.

"Teaston, don't run away."

"I'm not…"

"That's all you do, run away from yourself."

"I told Marcel."

"But did you tell him that you also want to jump?"

"Who says I want to jump?"

"Teaston."

"I only want…"

"Teaston, I saw your paintings. There's a yearning in them. I saw death, yours maybe, but mainly other people's death."

"You saw my death."

"No, Teaston, I saw your face."

"I don't have a face, like I don't have a name. I'm nothing."

"You cannot see beyond the whiteness."

"How do you know about the whiteness?"

"I know. It's all around you."

The blind old man gets up and walks away. He carries a long aluminum cane in front of him. But somehow, the tip of the cane never touches the ground, the curbs, or the walls. He moves as if he has memorized every street, every angle. He seems to know every corner of Cassis as he knows the corners of my spirit.

I watch him walk one block and turn the corner at Rue Frédéric Mistral. What if I forget about him? After all, he is only a blind old man with the skin the color of burnt umber. No, he may know things about me that I do not know. I cannot let him go, not now. I run after him but when I turn the same corner, I find the street empty, his figure lost somewhere. Where? Where? I walk down the street looking for him. Nothing. I enter the first open establishment, Café Alizé, and stare at the faces of men and women who in turn stare at me in bewilderment. Why do they look at me with such intensity? A stale woman behind the bar asks me if I want a drink or something like that. Her words tumble; eat each other like hungry crocodiles, leaving bloody corpses on top of the mahogany bar. Move on, he must be here. I go to the back of the Café where a dim light bulb hangs naked from the ceiling.

Light, light.

I look inside the men's toilet. He is not here. But when I step out of the toilet, I see the shadow of the blind old man leaving through the front door of the café, back into the whiteness of the street. Through the web of looks I cross the length of the café and exit into the street.

A resplendent emptiness.

Steps.

I hear steps moving away from me, down the street.

Tip, tap, tip, tap.

I try to catch up with the steps but they continue to move ahead of me.

Tip, tap, tip.

They are still ahead.

Tip, ton, tip, ton.

I run faster down the street.

Teas, tap, teas, tap.

Faster, faster.

Teas, tip, teas, ton, teas.

I see a silhouette casting an oblique shadow on the sidewalk. Can words cast shadows?

Teas, tap, ton, tip, teas, ton, tap, tip.

What am I hearing?

Ton, ton, teas, ton, teas, ton.

I run fast trying to grab the shadow, the words.

From someone's mouth, "Teaston, Teaston, Teaston."

Nothing

In the mornings she walks away.

In the afternoons she listens.

Bluish scars cross her back. When I learned about those I trembled. I do not look at those scars now; I only look at her face.

She seems aware of my apprehension, my disorganized thoughts. She also knows that I am afraid. When I enter the studio with my face burning, she knows I touched reality. And my reality is very close to death. She gives me space and time, and only talks to me when I am ready. When I am confused, or afraid, she soothes me with her silence.

I approach her while she sits at the edge of our bed. She knows I am conflicted about something, that my mind is turning. When I clear the white smoke from my eyes and manage to think as straight as I can, I resolve to speak to her.

"I feel like I don't know."

"You don't, Teaston."

"I want to understand what's really happening."

"I want the same thing."

"Camila, what keeps you from knowing?"

"You do."

"No, no, I don't."

"You walk around as if you were dead."

"I'm not dead."

"No, you're not dead for the moment."

"Do you know when will I die?"

"No, Teaston, only you know that."

Camila kisses my forehead, and I feel as if her lips extract the thoughts out of my head. She pulls those loose filaments of broken logic and spreads them out for the wind to disperse. I hear my thoughts bouncing from wall to wall, unbridled, revealing my fears, anger, and shame.

I need to hold on, to feel the weight of her body. I hear words coming out of her mouth and hope those words will bind me. When she speaks, her words twirl and twist in the air and become entangled with my thoughts. I want to grab them, to make a beautiful bouquet to plant in the center of my brain. But the wind carries the words away, and my thoughts, and everything.

As I lean over the edge of the bed I reach the point of vertigo, the divisive line, the verge of life and death, of real and unreal. With my right hand digging the mattress and my feet up in the air, I barely cling, avoiding contact with the floor. My penis hangs loose over the cliff, far away from Camila's reach. She leans back on the bed and watches as I struggle to keep my balance. I think she is talking but I cannot hear what she says. I can only hear my thoughts broadcast to the houses nearby, to the old port, to the universe. So naked.

My skull must be porous, or maybe the thoughts just come out of my mouth, like projectile vomit. I try to hold on to them, to rein them back into my mind. But no, they just pour out of me like a flooded river. Camila laughs; she says she never knew I feared Marcel. I do, but I will never say it. She then becomes serious; she must have heard me think about death or about asking her to die with me.

Nude, my mind denuded.

I pull my body back into the center of the bed and lay my head on Camila's abdomen. Her abdomen feels soft, the silky texture of her white skin molds around my head. She smells of fresh linen. I rest, wanting nothing more than rest. And Camila knows what I need, for she stays silent watching me breathe. She caresses my forehead while singing a simple lullaby. Her words flutter around me, while I hope my thoughts of death go unnoticed to her, and to the world.

When I close my eyes I see the world. I see the whiteness and many faces that come rushing in. I cannot paint them. Camila knows I see faces, but that does not bother her. No, she loves me more for that. Like she does this minute, caressing me and singing, isolating me from myself.

Resting, or sleeping, or just breathing—anything else but thinking. I must avoid thinking now. Like when I first knew my mind was confused, a young man I was, and my mother's hand swatted the intrusive thoughts away. I did not think about death then, I only thought about not thinking. How white.

I try to eviscerate my mind. I want to see nothing, hear nothing; I only want to feel her touch. But the image of Phillipy invades me. I bring my knees to my chest, wrap my arms around my legs, and bend my head. Phillipy flutters over me. I rock myself. I am a fetus, a newborn, a child in fear, a young man who does not know why. I want nothing, maybe my death, but instead I get Phillipy's death. Why, why, why?

With my eyes closed, I reach for Camila's hand.

Nothing.

Camila, I need you. Where is your warmth?

I rock forcefully.

I do not dare to open my eyes. I thrash in the bed wanting to feel her skin.

Nothing.

I rock more. Nothing stops me from rocking.

Camila, talk to me.

Nothing.

Marcel, don't...

At my door. Where else but at my door? Marcel knocks softly and I listen to his knuckles as they crash against the wooden panels. Marcel is at my door knocking once, not three times as Phillipy used to knock. He wants to know what happened; he wants to hear from me. I also want to hear from myself because, sometimes, I surprise myself with my own discourse. Marcel keeps knocking at the door, not so softly.

When I open the door, I see Marcel standing outside with a cigarette in his mouth and a lost expression. He does not bring his typical energetic self with him. He seems to just be. That is all. I ask him to come inside and he does. I ask him to make himself comfortable and he does not. He carries sadness with him, like a heavy saddle. I ask him to tell me what bothers him. He sits on a stool in my studio and looks at me.

"What happened, Teaston?"

"I don't really know."

"You were there."

"Teaston was there."

"That's you."

"Most often."

"Why did he...?"

"I don't know."

"Did he say anything about his mother?"

"His mother?"

"Yes, his mother."

"What would he have said?"

"That she's dead."

"I'm dead, too."

"Teaston, c'mon."

"He couldn't even pronounce the word 'death'."

"I know, he wanted to find her."

"He did."

"Where did he find her?"

"On the other side."

"Teaston…"

"On the other side, the side that he couldn't pronounce."

Marcel knows I am talking about death. He knows that Phillipy wanted to find his mother. He knows that his mother meant death to him. But he does not know he wanted to paint her, or to find her in his painting. Marcel does not know that Phillipy painted his dead mother or that he painted me with death all around. He thinks Phillipy came to my studio to learn how to paint, when in reality, Phillipy came to my studio to learn how to die. However, I did not teach him how to die—he already knew.

"What did he say at the end?"

"He called his mother."

"How do you know?"

"He called, *Maman*."

"Did he call for me?"

"Marcel, you are not dead."

Marcel is not dead, and he represented life for Phillipy. But life is what Phillipy had, not what he craved. He longed for the other side; he wanted to paint the dead. He painted me as a dead man, or simply as he saw me, dead indeed. He also painted the little death, Lucio. And at the end he painted his mother in her glorious death. She must have been real to him for he leaped to touch her, to join with her.

Marcel does not know what Phillipy really wanted. He possibly never understood him well. A child that never became a man, a man that behaved like a child, a mind confined inside its own mind, a person who ignored other persons, an impossible painter, a boy who wanted to join with death, a motherless child. And when Marcel asks about Phillipy, I can only say that I know nothing, or that I am not sure, for the truth is that I do not really know much about Phillipy.

"They want to talk to you, Teaston."

"Who wants to talk to me?"

"The *gendarmes*."

"Why do they insist in wasting their time?"

"You seem to be close to people before they fall off the cliff."

"But I haven't fallen off."

"That's exactly why they want to talk to you."

"I'm not a murderer. I'm nothing."

"But you've been there."

"Marcel, do you think I killed your boy?"

"No, Teaston."

No, I did not kill his boy. I have not killed anyone. I was there, yes. Present, maybe. Like I have been every time I considered jumping myself. Somehow, I am present when people make life and death decisions. They had a death wish, but don't we all?

Marcel walks around my studio breathing the air that Phillipy breathed at the end. He looks at the walls, the northern window, the accumulation of unfinished canvases, the collection of paint tubes, and the air of worldly failure. I doubt he understands anything about painting, but he understands something about life. He serves wine, he serves life— he must have served death. He turns to me on his way out of the studio.

His right eye…!

"Marcel, he wanted to join her."

"I wanted to join her too."

"What, Marcel?"

"I always thought of the sea."

"No, not in that way."

"What do you mean?"

"The way of loneliness."

"Well, I don't have him and I don't have her."

"Marcel, don't…"

The waves are impatient

Do not.

Do not do.

Do not do what will dissolve.

Do not do what will dissolve your memory and render you as what you are not, or at least as what you will not want to be, or what your own memory will not allow. I refuse to be remembered as a killer, for I am not one. At the edge of the cliff there are many forces that play into the gravity of the moment. Murder is not one of them.

Murder.

From someone's mouth, "Murderer."

A painter, perhaps.

With my name on my shoulders, and the weight of the fallen, I decide to follow the trail down to the sea. The very trail Camila helped me traverse, one of her many paths, but a path that brings me to the point of death, the contact point with the rocks before the sea. That must be the moment when death occurs.

From someone's mouth, "Murderer."

No, painter. I am a painter.

The sea comes in a forceful way, on, and on, and on, spreading foam and salt all over when it bursts onto the rocks. The sea aims to destroy the rocks; it tries to expose their solid meanness. This is my own body, the sea, and I am stunned by the fierce temper and the resolve to crush the rocks. Does it want to kill? Do I want to kill? A murderer—the sea.

I am a painter.

But what I need to paint eludes me. The faces kissed the rocks before joining my body. I try to render them in hues of green, blue, or gray, Greco distorted but recognizable; and I continue to fail, having to throw white foam all over them. I see them now, hoping to stay, but the white paint and the foam swallow them.

The faces lose their form at the point of impact with the rocks. From this moment onwards, we only have a memory of what the contours looked like. I have my memories. What happens next is a mystery. My body is implicated but I do not know how. A receiving vastness, engulfing, or a drowning terminator, a wet graveyard. I do not know.

With no blood traces to mark the last moment with certainty, I can only guess where death happened. I try to smell it, but the salt spray erases all vestiges of conflict. If life screamed, the roar of the sea against the rocks would have silenced it. No traces, a continuous flush of my body over the rocks, no traces.

I found the olive woman's necklace among the rocks, the shining amulet that conjures whiteness. I may find more of them here. If Phillipy were to leave a relic, this would be the place. Although I did not see the trajectory of his fall, Phillipy must have graced the rocks. I can sense his presence here. Death it is, just death. Marcel said nothing about his body being intact or distorted. But I know these rocks would have claimed something. I can feel it.

From someone's mouth, "Murderer."

I taught him, I did not kill him.

My body rages. The waves advance throwing themselves with impetus

Swim, Teaston, swim

From the rocks, bleeding, I ascend to my studio. I follow the same path that led me down to the place of transformation. I rise leaving a trail of blood behind. And as the air gets thinner, the voices travel faster, growing to occupy the entirety of my skull. I deposit my bruised body on the bare floor of my studio. The voices take advantage of my weakened self to rampage through my mind.

"Bring Teaston forward."

"What?"

"Bring the bastard in."

"Who?"

"Turn yourself in."

"Myself?"

"Yes, you bastard."

I can present myself, or whatever is left of myself—I can bring that forward. Yes, I will find you and you will have me. I am coming. As I prepare to descend to the old port Camila pulls me back into my studio. This is her hour, I can tell. She looks at me, wet, blood running down my back, her eyes showing deep tenderness. She makes me stay on the bare floor and begins to caress the back of my head.

"Teaston."

"The waves, Camila, the waves."

"Are you hurt?"

"My body is hurt; the rest of me is dying."

"Where are you going, Teaston?"

"They want me to bring myself forward."

"Teaston, who?"

"I don't know."

I tell her they summoned me by my name. She calls me by that name, so does Marcel, and Phillipy, no longer, and Her Horrible Majesty, and over the rocks, retreating, charging again, and heading back through the crevices, the cracks, before joining the core of my body. And over again. The foam, white and hollow, floats over the rocks, insubstantial, masking the place of death. My forceful body pulls me, it wants to drag my feet, it wants to make me fall into myself.

I watch as the size of the waves increases with the coming of the tide. The moon pulls my body up the rocks. And with every charge, the sea claims me further. The seagulls know I am struggling, and they laugh. But I stand, wet and cold, over the place of impact, the last ground before the fallen fell deeper. I need to save this piece of rock as a sanctuary, the place where faces change; the impact, the tearing of the skin, the crushing of orbital bones and mandibles. All I know about the faces of the fallen changed in this spot.

The waves charge.

Against me, from the vastness of my body comes a force that brings me to my knees. From behind me, the retreating force drags me over the rocks. I feel a hardness against the back of my head, a dull crack, as my vision becomes blurred, and the foam turns pink. Again. Again. Again. I look up to the sky but find no blue in it, only a faint darkness.

The rocks cradle me. The sea wants to reclaim its own, pulling, pulling. My mouth becomes silent when flooded.

And the seagulls above.

Surrounded by foam my mind seeks to comprehend. Am I sinking? Is my blood draining away? Why can't I move? Could this be my end?

Camila, this is the path you take when you disappear from me in the mornings. Maybe this is not your hour. But this is my hour. I will walk up the hill with you. Walk by me, come to me, Camila; the dead are not here, you do not need to fear their presence. The only death to see is mine. Come soon, Camila, the waves are impatient.

the *gendarmes*, and the blind old man, and everybody in this world who has a claim on my existence. Now someone calls me to validate my existence, as Teaston.

"Nobody is calling you, Teaston."

"They are asking for Teaston to come forward."

"But who's asking?"

"I'll find out when I get there."

"Where are you going?"

"I don't know."

"Teaston."

"I'm not Teaston, who cares?"

"I care."

"In the afternoon."

"Isn't this our time?"

"Your time, Camila. Mine is ending."

How will I face those who demand to see me right away? Maybe they only want to ask the time of day, or maybe they want to see that Teaston exists. A big disappointment they face, for I will not answer any questions, not about the cliff, not about Phillipy.

Derailed, I descend, I swim, I walk, I move towards the old town. Such a place sleeps on its back and people walk all over it. I walk over a path known to me, the street leading to Marcel's restaurant, the corner hosting the blind old man, he is not there, the quay, the image of Her Majesty. Without Camila, alone and exposed to whatever this wretched town can foist into me, I move towards the old port. The thought of being a ghost is thrilling, and I embrace it, thinking that my ghost is only a shallow transparency, a gesture offering nothing.

Through the streets I walk. I extend my arms in a global embrace longing to hug the universe. I want to pull all the souls into my body. I want my body to swell with the dreams and desires of everyman. But no... all I feel is a mediocre pull, a simulacrum of the truth, an empty search for nothingness, in prose, in painting. I need to fill my body with the words of the rebels. But the rebels are asleep, tired of their duty, unaffected by the hunger for a new order. I will then push my concepts and ideas against the canon of the moment. But against the *gendarmes,* my ideas are like water, fluid and inconsistent. I come to the old port to talk about my body, not about my mind. I fall back into the darkness of the day and accept their version of the game.

I hear a few steps behind me.

I stop.

Nothing.

Ahead, let me walk ahead, I can play their game. The steps again, faint first but now more pronounced.

I stop.

Calm.

I am bringing myself forward, but where should I deliver myself?

The steps.

The steps catch up with me. On my left I see a short man, on my right, another man, but tall and bearded. They walk at my same pace while looking ahead, not at me. We walk like this for about half a block when, all the sudden, both men come closer to me until the point where our elbows touch.

"This is him."

"Are you sure?"

"Yes, just look at him."

At this point they each grab one of my arms and take off running down the street. First I run with them, squeezed in between their bodies, but then I try to stop. They do not stop; they keep their speed dragging my body along, like a twig. After a few turns, we reach a quiet corner of the old port where they drop my body on the floor by the seawall.

"I'm bringing myself forward."

"Yes, Teaston, we know."

With a piece of string they try to tie my feet together. The clumsy short man cannot make a proper knot. The tall bearded man pushes him aside and makes a better knot. He then ties my hands behind my back.

"I'm not Teaston."

"Then, why did you bring yourself forward?"

The tall bearded man lifts me by my shoulder blades while the short man barely lifts my legs. At the count of three, they dump my body into the sea.

"Swim, Teaston, swim."

My ruby strokes

She finds me wet and bloody. But what can be expected after swimming and crashing against the rocks? To my surprise, I still breathe, air flows into my lungs while a white frothy substance leaks out of my nose. She caresses my back; Camila does, and wipes clean my dripping nose.

"This is our time, Teaston."

I do not know what time this is. How can I tell when the world keeps changing in front of my eyes? I almost drowned a few minutes ago, before that, I hit hard rocks with my soft body. And Camila there, present to soothe me. How does she find me at this very time? She, who walks all around the shore, the cliffs, the town, absent from me, or anyone, how does she know when to come? She does, like she knew when to walk up the hill with me. How does she call that time? Was that our time?

I am bleeding. I feel a sticky dampness on the back of my head. I touch the wetness with my fingers and admire the dark ruby color of my blood. Blood drips fresh, warm, and real. It pours; it bathes my broken body, this solid body of mine.

Dark.

Dark ruby.

Dark ruby red.

I reach for one of the canvases covered by multiple layers of failure, the very top layer all white now. I find my balance and mount the canvas at a low point in the easel standing in front of me. Phillipy used this easel. He painted from inside himself. When I sit on the floor, facing the canvas, I can hear him call "*Maman*."

"Phillipy, I'm dead and you knew it."

My right hand reaches behind my head and dips my fingers into the gash. The layers of skin open up to reveal a beefy ravine, a violation of the integrity of my body, an entry into my head. There is no pain now. With my fingers I enter my head, scooping ruby red. I start to lay down lines on the white canvas, painting what lives inside of me with what comes from inside me.

The shape of almond eyes, a mouth, whose chin? The curvature of the cheekbones. An expression, begging for rescue or begging for death. A yearning for a name, a yearning for a mother, a yearning for being everyone, or everyone dead, a yearning for a body, fluid, extensive. I bring my fingers back to the source of paint, again and again, digging deeper, scooping as much red as possible.

Who are you?

I render a long face. Man or woman? A dead face; eyes closed, mouth distorted. Who are you? The face ignores me. I want to recognize, identify the face my fingers paint, but its identity eludes me. My fingers jump, adding a small detail here, another shadow there. A shade under the eyes, a wrinkle. But the face flees from me.

"This is our time, Teaston."

The lights ditch me as well, and a shadow or a gray curtain falls over me. Camila. The air becomes incorporeal, unable to sustain my breathing. Camila. A tingling sensation reaches the tip of my fingers. Camila. And my spine begins to cave under the weight of my body.

My painting stays incomplete. A red rendering showing nothing other than my own questions, or my own fears about who they are, the ones that are no longer, and even more disturbing, the ones that hound me, or try to do me harm.

"Our time, Camila."

Weakness floods my body as blood ebbs out of my mind, or paint, or memories, or images of those I can no longer recognize. But my right hand needs to keep painting, spreading ruby over the canvas. But, no, no more. And before I collapse on the floor, trembling, I regurgitate white foam, brilliant, luminous, covering the newly born redness, erasing all of my ruby strokes.

Touch my body now

"He wasn't my son."

"Of course not, who said he was?"

"Marcel, he wasn't my son."

"I know. He was *my* son."

"Yes."

"Yes, Teaston."

Marcel agrees with me on this issue of whose son Phillipy was. How could I even consider that Phillipy was my son? I do not know, but somehow, I thought he was. My mind, chaotic, fabricates that kind of relationships. Like water and flesh, or blood and paint.

"He was my only son."

"You can have more sons if you want to."

"I don't want to have any more."

"Good."

"What's so good about it?"

"You will learn to forget."

Marcel finishes cleaning the bar while I empty my glass of red wine. I do not like staying here this late but Marcel insists. He wants company, I suppose. Maybe he needs to cry. I have not seen him cry yet, not even when the *gendarmes* showed him the disfigured Phillipy. What kind of father is Marcel? With a son like Phillipy, what kind of father is he? These late hours are abusive. I am sure Phillipy did not like for his father to work late at night. But he never spoke about his father. And Marcel barely speaks about Phillipy, or Phillipy's mother, the woman on the other side.

"I'm almost finished. Do you want another glass?"

"Yes."

Putting the red back into my mind, I drink slowly, watching Marcel. We never speak about anything. Yet, the constant presence of his eye fluttering above the serving tray and the constant presence of my body sitting at my table, these elements bring us together. This is why I wait for him now, late at night, when I should be hiding from those who wish to hurt me.

Marcel grabs a bottle of wine and two glasses from the bar, turns the lights off, and asks me to wait outside while he closes the restaurant. We then walk toward the seawall and sit on a half-rotten bench.

"I've nothing, Teaston."

"I don't know what to say."

"There's nothing to say."

We drink. The sea talks to us in a low hoarse voice. My voice. My sea body is all black and supple, undulating, extending an embracing welcome. From the top of numerous masts, blinking eyes look upon us.

I wonder if Marcel knows the sea. He knows death. The woman who bore Phillipy turned into death. Phillipy brought death to him. So Marcel must have thought about it, he must have considered joining them. We drink.

"What keeps you here, Teaston?"

"I need to paint faces."

"Is that enough?"

"No. I need to paint everyman's face, the face of the dead."

"What about living people? Do you like people?"

"Some people, almost nobody."

"I see people all day in the restaurant, and I don't like them."

"Did Phillipy like people?"

"He liked you. But he said you were dead. That kid had strange ideas."

"Marcel, do you think I'm dead?"

"No. Do you want to be?"

"Sometimes."

"Yes, I feel the same."

No more words. My irresolute self, oozing death and not living up to it. Let the sea speak instead with its unanimous sound. A vaster, more authoritative voice. Let the crash of the waves explain my disappointment, my solitude. In Marcel's face I see a need for words, but the sea does not speak for him. He has not embodied his yearning and the inevitable transmigration into nature. His is a young journey.

"What do you live for, Marcel?"

"I don't know anymore."

"Can you see yourself as a dead person?"

"I don't know what that would be like."

"Do you want to be dead?"

"I don't know, Teaston."

"I think about it all the time, night and day."

"Is that why you drink so much?"

"No, that's to drown the voices."

"What voices?"

"There are no voices, there's only death."

"You've thought of killing yourself, haven't you?"

"I don't trust death. That's my problem."

"Are you afraid of death?"

"I'm not afraid of death. It's the loneliness after death that frightens me."

That is my problem. A fear of death as a reckless force, an erratic

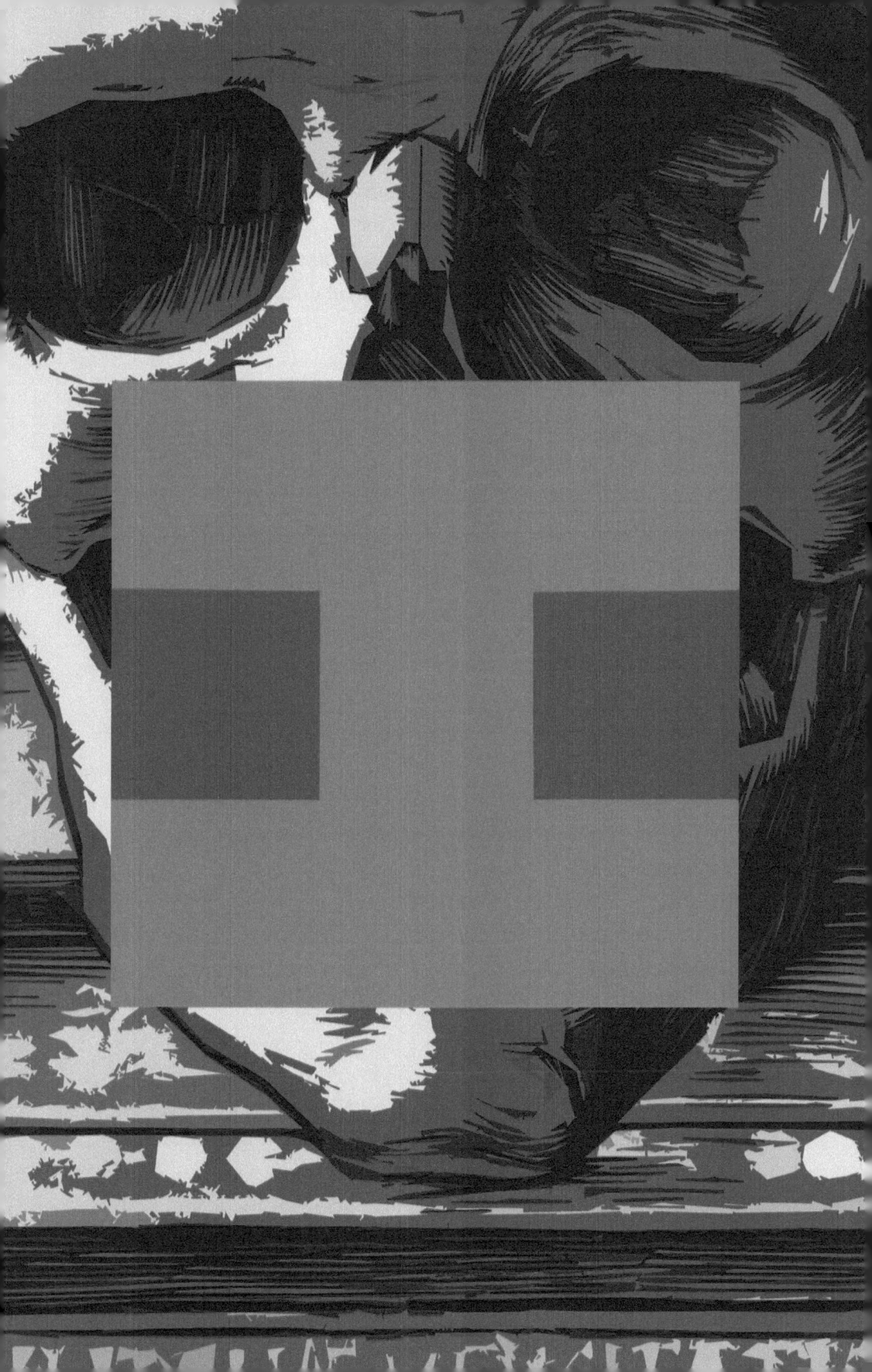

fulminating power set on ending it all. I crave to end the life of Teaston, but I hate to stop existing in some form, the sea, maybe. But death, no, death is confused, and my right hand seems aware, for it holds on to the ground every time I gaze over the edge. Marcel does not know the edge; he is a fresh death-wisher. We drink more.

"Are you alone, Marcel?"

"Yes."

"Nobody there?"

"No, just like you, I think."

"I've Camila, sometimes I do."

"Who's Camila?"

"You've seen her…"

"No, you're always alone."

"She sits at my table."

"You're always alone, Teaston."

"Camila sits with me."

"You're alone, just like me. That's why I bring glasses of Bandol to your table."

Marcel does not believe in Camila. But I do. I need her. Do not walk away now, Camila. Not know. I am alone and the thought of death penetrates my mind. I am dripping paint. My porous mind cannot hold my thoughts. I am dripping. Soon there will be nothing more of me. I need you to laugh, to kiss my right hand. Camila, come and touch me, touch my body now.

I touch her

My studio knows how to breathe. Without me, my studio knows to hold its breath until the next calamity. I may damage my own paintings, foaming over them, painting them white. I may invite souls like Phillipy who would ransack the place. I could also abandon the studio and let the winter freeze any sign of life. So impotent the space, like the desert, open to all the forces. I coalesce here, my life from before and my current failures. This temple burns in its own desire, it burns.

The northern window allows the light I need. How else? The paint knows to laugh when the window opens wide. The light and the paint vibrate, holding each other, like lovers do. And when I come determined to paint faces, the lovers scowl and turn away from me. There is death around me, I know, and the northern light agrees. That is why I turn my face southward, to the sun and the sea, towards the cliff.

Today burns like petroleum, as my right hand prepares to paint. Today I will render the face of everyman, the death mask of the fallen. We all fall from the inside, day by day, until the final leap. I will paint a tribute to that moment, an image to remember.

I prepare to paint.

I pull out all my brushes, painting knives, wooden palette, turpentine, rags, and oil tubes in cobalt violet, gold ochre, Venetian red, warm sepia, burnt umber, and a very deep cerulean blue. I grab one of my defunct canvases and place it on the easel where the northern light drenches it. I sit in front of this arrangement.

The memories march in the horizon, like a battalion of wounded soldiers. Slowly, they approach me swinging their weapons and yelling obscenities. The faces I painted in the past fly over me and I feel parts of them, an ear, or a tongue, brushing my cheek. I hear people talk.

No!

Stop now!

I need to paint.

I mix the oils quickly and start to paint at once, hoping to squelch the assault. I quickly lose track of what to paint but my right hand seems to know. My hand moves fast, brushing pigments unto the canvas, hurting it with cadmium red, caressing it with viridian green, stroking it with raw sienna. The gestures are ancient, desperate attempts to create life on the canvas. I abandon myself to the movement of my hand and the illusion of creation. There is only one space now, one consciousness.

Paint drips from inside my mind.

The movement of the sea, the waves, the feeling of one continuous body, extending to the curvature ahead. There is no Teaston now, nor the man who is not Teaston. The dead are no longer. Only this oceanic feeling exists. Who creates? Who is rendered? Who is the observer?

My hand paints as if joined to the body of a different artist, a Toledan master from the 16th century. And from the whiteness of the canvas, a figure emerges. The traces bring to light two elongated eyes full of sorrow, downcast, as if longing for someone. The mouth... not yet, there is no mouth. The curve of the face, delicate, with a fine chin, reveals the profile of a woman. Now the forehead, in pale tonalities.

Below her are the world, St. Martina and St. Agnes, a lamb, and a docile lion who stares at me. Two cherubs flank her. Her mouth now, closed, the lips touching each other softly, in peaceful acceptance. A small mouth.

A naked man/child emerges in the forefront of the composition. All flesh, thick thighs, and a head crowned with golden hair. His right hand grabs the index finger of the woman while his eyes seem to look into the distance, away from everything. The man/child is not in touch with this world, he inhabits his own.

Could she be my mother? No, my mother was distant; she never grabbed my hand. I do not know what it feels to have a mother. But this woman I am painting is someone's mother, a suffering one. She molds her body to the weight of the man/child, her dreams too. But I detect certain coldness about the man/child, with his diaphanous skin and his disdain for her touch. She seems to feel his emotional absence, but she loves him nonetheless.

I have seen this woman. She may be dead but her image exists somewhere. Hers is an angelic presence, not a haunting one, an image I have encountered before. Where can I find this Madonna and Child?

Would she want to be my mother?

I stop painting. I need to find her. Through my entire studio I search for a lost painting. But there are no photographs or picture books in my studio. I only keep human images in my memory, that erratic depository damaged by the whiteness. I look everywhere.

Nothing.

I come across the hardbound book that I resist reading. No, not this book. But what if there is a picture in there? I should not read this book. But I need to look inside; I need to find that picture. Turning my face away from it, I hold the book by its covers and shake it to allow the pages to open up. Nothing falls from the book. I close the book at once and place it on top of the table. I do not want to open that book again.

One painting. Is there a painting or an image somewhere in this studio? I then remember the painting Phillipy made of his mother before he jumped from the cliff. I know I brought it to my studio. But I never saw the painting; my mind did not see that painting, my thoughts were derailed then. I rush to my stack of white canvases and pull out the painting I rescued from the cliff, Phillipy's masterpiece.

I let the northern light reveal the painting. I see the same mother with elongated eyes full of sorrow, downcast, as if longing for someone. Below her is the world, St. Martina and St. Agnes, a lamb and a docile lion. A naked man/child grabs her finger.

Phillipy wanted to touch her again.

I extend my arm and touch the image with my fingers.

I touch her.

She thought I was crazy

She is my mother.

She is not my mother.

She is not what my mother would have been.

But how do I know what my mother would have been if she herself was not around to show me, to care for me in the most basic way, to comfort me when the fears started, when the voices accusing me replaced her soft voice and tried to convince me to jump or to cut my veins open or to walk under the fast approaching train when I should have been playing, away from harm's way, just playing with the other children that never saw a thing and never heard their own thoughts broadcast, playing the games full of logic and consequences, the very games I could play then but not today, for my mind feels neglected and this recent view of a mother only serves to derail my thoughts, I can see how my thoughts jump

jump

and the water

my body

the warm desire to fly over the rocks, missing them, landing straight into my own body, and swimming away

with you, Camila

even if you walk away from me in the mornings

my hand says hello, it wants to paint, it paints what I cannot paint

all the dead faces

even my face

does Teaston have a face?

and Tuesday burns like petroleum

my face burning

my eye intact while Marcel's eye flutters, his eye

under me the sea, above an uncertain future, the sea

the white wall, the white mattress, the

when, not yet, only after all is lost or forgotten

Camila, no, she walks

I feel the rock when it enters my head, blood is inevitable

hello blood

and if I were to

killing is not part of my repertoire
the cliff, thanks
let me be another, when Teaston is gone
not me, not me in a hundred years, better dead
death, pretty, isn't she
isn't she? maybe, because it isn't me
the book wants to say
not to me, I am not the book
being, something, being, nothing
nothing, nothing, nothing, nothing, nothing, nothing
yes, Teaston
never heard you say "I"
feel the pain now

I feel the pain now, the pain of my mind breaking down, the sore muscles of my brain trying to reign the thoughts in, trying to hold on, a desire no longer possible, a road abandoned long time ago, perhaps before the whiteness. My mother, did she know about the pain? Did she know why I spoke like a lunatic, why I could not play with the other children who found me weird? Did she leave me because she could not understand? Did she run away from me because she thought I was crazy?

Marcel looking at me

The blind old man is blind.

He stands by my side, smokes a cigarette, and turns his head around as if watching the pretty girls parading down the seafront. In fact, most people know that he is old—but very few know that he is blind. He has a mind like no other. A whole life of darkness has not deadened his luminous vibrancy. He orchestrates the life of the quay, he participates in every conversation, and he can sense motives and desires. Even when people ignore him, a bum, a *clochard*, they call him, he picks up on their fears. He can sense the tension in their voices, the desolation in the unspoken words.

He is blind.

Today he has a sense of urgency, one cigarette lights the next, and his feet keep shuffling, wanting to go somewhere. In the middle of this bright autumn day, the blind old man sweats profusely, even though he wears no scarf, even though a cold breeze blows from the sea. Every pore of his faces spurts a torrent of sweat. With the cigarette butt almost burning his fingers, he stares at me.

"Why did you hide it from me, Teaston?"

"What?"

"The Madonna and Child."

"I haven't hidden anything."

"I went to your studio and you didn't show her to me."

"You mean, Phillipy's painting."

"No, Teaston, your painting."

"I painted a woman, but that was only yesterday."

"Your mother, Teaston?"

"No, Phillipy's mother."

"Above the world, with the cherubs flanking her, and the man/child on her bosom?"

"Have you seen the painting?"

"No, but I know it was painted a long time ago."

"She's not my mother."

"How do you know that?"

"It was Phillipy who painted her before he jumped."

"Are you also going to jump after her?"

"She's not my mother."

"Whose son are you, Teaston?"

"I'm not Teaston."

"I'm not blind."

No more. I stay a few feet away from him and hold my breath. I become utterly silent, dead silent. And I watch how the blind old man moves his head right and left trying to sense my presence, to sniff my body.

No air.

He then fixes his wooden eyes in my direction and grins, an ample grin, mischievous even.

Gasping from inside.

"I can hear your thoughts, Teaston."

Silence. No air.

"Why are they so jumbled?"

No air.

"She's above the world, Teaston, yours and Phillipy's."

I breathe again and air comes roaring in, a maddening gust of oxygen, nitrogen, and saltpeter, vibrating, desperately filling every little pocket in my lungs. My body has no gills. I am above the surface and he can tell that I am breathing air. Even worse, he can hear my thoughts.

"My hand painted her face, and everything around her."

"Your hand?"

"Yes, my right hand."

"My eyes can see your right hand."

"No, they cannot."

"Neither can your hand paint someone else's painting."

"I didn't paint someone else's painting."

"There's is only one Madonna, Teaston."

"I think I painted her."

"Is it different from Phillipy's painting?"

"No."

"Your thoughts, Teaston, they lie."

My thoughts, that fluid current that smashes against rocks, jumping and sputtering around, uncontained and illogical. They grow, as people do, and die continuously. Their death an easier one, unlike mine, wished but unattainable. An arrow—a straight shot—they are not. But these are the thoughts I have. I live the life of my thoughts, a life of lies.

"Come with me, Teaston."

"Where?"

"To see the faces."

The blind old man offers me his arm and I grab on to him. He starts walking away from the quay, through the meandering streets that penetrate the old town. I let him lead me. We turn corners, dodge low awnings, step around fire hydrants, and at one point, he even kicks an insulting dog. We reach an ordinary building on an ordinary street. He stops outside the entrance and remains still and quiet; he seems to survey the smells, the sounds.

"There's no one around. We can go in."

All in one movement, the blind old man opens the lock with his key, pushes the door, and drags me inside. He closes the door behind us softly, like a whisper, and I am certain that nobody saw or heard us enter the building. Inside the foyer there is an inky darkness. I grab his arm tightly.

"Follow me."

"I can't see."

"Follow me."

The blind old man leads me up a set of stairs, one landing, two landings, three, perhaps. We walk along a dark corridor hardly illuminated by a faint light filtering from under a closed door. I hear some voices. Whose voices? He finally stops in front of the closed door and rests. He lights a cigarette, and the glow of the flame creates intangible shadows.

"Close your eyes, Teaston; I'm going to open the door."

He opens the door.

Light, light, emanates from the walls. So intense a whiteness. A white air seems to embrace my body, eating at my flesh with luminous intensity. A sense of drowning. My right hand squeezes his arm until I hear him moan.

"I'm right here, Teaston."

"This is…"

"Don't say anything; just wait until you can see."

"The light hurts my eyes."

"Yes, I know."

A shade dies, and then another, but the thickness of the milky air seems unending. I force myself to remain static, letting the veils fall. And like a procession, the shadows and contrasts march in conjuring a vision of faces along a gallery of wide and tall walls. Aligned in meticulous rows, I see the paintings, the faces I failed to paint.

"These were my paintings."

"They *are* your paintings, Teaston."

"I painted them over with white paint."

"This is a white room."

"But, they're all dead."

"The people, but not their faces. You know that, Teaston."

They are all here. The paintings of my past before the whiteness. Even the more recent one, the olive woman with her oblong eyes, is here. There are many versions of her, all the same, all different. And Lucio, the little death, dying over and over again in his innocence. Also the elusive everyman under every possible light, with every possible expression before death. And Phillipy, avoiding the viewers' eyes, as if looking into his own world.

"These are all my paintings."

"Not all of them. I'm missing The Madonna."

"My last painting?"

"It may be your last, or it may not."

"But nobody can see these paintings; they don't even exist."

"They do, Teaston. Can't you see how luminous they are?"

I run.

Into the dark corridor I run. Touching the walls to avoid falling, I feel my way until my hands grab on to the stair railing.

Tip, tap, tip, tap.

The blind old man follows me.

Teas, tip, teas, ton, teas.

I descend the stairs until I cannot go down any further.

Teas, tap, ton, tip, teas, ton, tap, tip.

Here, at the bottom of the darkness, I try to find the exit.

Ton, ton, teas, ton, teas, ton.

A way out of my mind.

I know when to run and this is one of those times. Past the multiple doors and windows, over cobblestones, there is the sea. Always the sea. And determined to face my body, I keep running until the street ends at the seawall. This edge is the dividing line between me and more of me. I come to rest in front of the vastness, dotted by boats of all sizes, seagulls too.

"I'm here."

Leaning against the seawall, Her Majesty watches as I come to an abrupt stop. She insists in swallowing me, she wants to draw my attention— she wants to eat my mind. And without looking at her, I sit at the seawall and hope my skull will be solid enough to keep her away.

"Teaston."

"Die now, you whore."

"Easy, son, easy."

No… This is not she. This is not Her Majesty. This is some other nightmare trying to make me upset. I am not looking; I am not giving in to this crazy voice. I said "crazy." She said "crazy," my mother did. No, she did not mean to say that.

"Little Teaston of mine, drink from me."

"Die, bitch."

"Watch who you call bitch."

"Go away."

Her Majesty unbuttons her filthy shirt and exposes her breasts, large, engorged. She positions herself right in front of me and sways from side to

side, her breasts making a *demi lune* pattern in the afternoon light.

"Drink from me."

"I don't need you."

"My boy."

"I'm not your boy."

"Little Teaston, put your lips right here."

No. No. No. The sea rises, or maybe the waves, but my body seems to come to a crest of sorts, a moment of anxious anguish, a sense of panic. I close my eyes and hope that Her Majesty will vanish, implode, die in front of me, or at least cover her breasts and stop taunting me. Her Majesty is a bitch. But then, so was… No, I am not thinking that thought; I am not violating her memory.

Enough.

She needs to die. I am not a murderer. I look around me for an object to throw at her. I will destroy her. But I am not a murderer. She is the one killing me. A stone, I grab it. I fling the stone as hard as I can but Her Majesty dodges it with mocking grace. Look for something larger, something lethal. Nothing.

"My breasts are bursting, Teaston. Come and suck."

"Leave me."

I resist looking her way. I resist killing her. I am not a murderer. Next to the boat ramp is a garbage bin full of life's residues. I kick it sideways and spill all its contents on the floor. Fish entrails, food remains, cans, dirty diapers, newspapers, cigarette butts, and two wine bottles empty of their soul. I grab one of the bottles by the neck and break it against the seawall. The jagged edge of the broken glass is promising.

Before she has a chance to back away, I swing the bottle trying to slash Her Majesty's throat. I miss. I wait for her to face me, and this time I really look at her, straight in her eyes, and launch a direct stab at her heart. She moves back in time to avoid the hit.

"Don't be naughty, Teaston."

"Die, you bitch."

"Here, kiss my nipples."

"Die now."

I swing at her with the broken bottle, again, and again. She dodges my attacks. I try to get closer but she moves away from me. She grabs both of her breasts and points the nipples directly at me. I drip paint.

A crowd forms a circle around me as if there is nowhere else to go. The gravity of so many eyes drags me down. But I do not let them deter me. I need to finish her. I ignore the crowd and throw my entire weight into a furious stab that misses Her Majesty again. I come to land over the scattered garbage and broken glass. My knees and elbows start to bleed. Then I feel the tremendous weight of a body landing over me, deflating my lungs, immobilizing me.

"Easy, Teaston."

"I'm not a murderer, but I need to kill her."

"There, there."

Two strong hands take the bottle away and turn me around. As I lie on the ground unable to move, I come to face that globe, that fluttering bloodshot eye of Marcel looking at me.

The combustion of my life

Ascending, from the filthy street, the garbage and the broken glass, up to my studio. Marcel drives my body to where he thinks it should rest, to where it may find some peace. The road twists in serpentine ways opening views to the sea, to the red tiles that keep people in Cassis dry and protected. My body bleeds a weak blood, nothing else. At the height of the cliff, my studio awaits. In its insignificant grandeur, my studio receives my body through the northern door, as it receives painterly light seeking a canvas on which to lie.

We enter the studio and I am surprised by the unfamiliarity, the

otherworldliness of the space. This is where I have painted the faces, this is where Phillipy has shown me how to paint, and this is where Camila has caressed me. This space, bathed in nubile gray, wanting to be yellow, hopes for a new hue to redeem itself.

Marcel knows some of the drips of paint on the floor are Phillipy's. He knows his son was as good a painter as I am. Am I a painter? He knows the man/child needed a place to regurgitate his own torturous thoughts. Phillipy knocked on my door, he painted from inside himself, and he bolted out, falling into an abyss that contained the genesis of himself. Phillipy was a visionary and a martyr, a demi-god, an imbecile who channeled my demonic thoughts as if they were his. Phillipy jumped and I have not. He is the better man.

I lie on the floor of the studio in spite of Marcel's insistence to bring me to my bed. I refuse any further help and ask Marcel to drop me right here, in the center of this tarnished place. I want to see the northern light penetrate my studio through the long rectangular window. And as soon as Marcel retreats, walks away, disappearing into the old road that leads him to the old town where he is swallowed by the crowd of people who want his wine and his damned eye, only then, I let my mind unravel.

Oh, no!

I have two hands. I have to hand. I have to and.

Kill the motherfucking appendix, that hand, the loose serpent that spits black ink at midnight.

The head of Medusa with its twirling fingers sticking up like hair.

Serpent, reptile.

The other hand is useless; it hangs at my side. Look at it, the lame other, a mirror image of the right one but without venom.

And so many women around me. And so many women are under me. And some women asunder. A sunder ling women rounding me.

I lift my head and stare at the women, all wanting to grab me. I need to warn them.

"I have no money for you."

"Go fuck yourself."

"I would if I could."

"Can't you?"

I want to touch them, slide my tongue between their thighs, but the moment I hear the solitude of my studio, I forget why I was at the old port or why I feel like a young adolescent with his penis between his hands.

"Prostitute."

"Don't say it."

The images, the irreverent thoughts, the logic disintegrating, the advance of a wave of chaos, sinking me.

At this time Camila. Over the rocky paths, or perhaps over the green carpet of moss, where the sun fails to kill. At this time Camila could be walking far away from me, or simply around the corner. In my studio, I wait for her. I have sweat and blood weaving a layer of disappointment over my scarred knees, my elbows. But I know she will clean my wounds, tell me I will be fine. She will walk with me to places I have yet to discover. Camila, come back from your walk, to the studio, to my side.

My neck.

Around my neck.

Around my neck, hanging, all in silver, a Bedouin necklace with beautiful old Mediterranean coral beads, black wooden prayer beads, and little crosses.

Where are you?

Through the drawers, cabinets, even the dark corners of my memory, I look for the Bedouin necklace until I find it sleeping without my neck. Let the weight of the necklace impart what it has to. Oblivious of how it hangs on me, I don the necklace without looking into the mirror this time. If there is eternal whiteness, so be it.

There is no Camila.

There is no Camila, yet.

And as I wait for her, a dense film of solitude descends over me. I want to escape, lift the corners of the film and step away. But there is no edge, no final limit. The film extends far beyond my imagination, and the only thing I fathom is nothingness, and the name of Teaston—one and the same.

I invoke a control I do not have. The ever-shifting world throws me into a lonely corner when I need someone. And when I crave solitude, my skull lets everybody into my mind. Thugs that beat me and royalty that flaunts breasts and vaginas surround me. No control over my hand, no control over my mind. And when I could almost touch Phillipy, he jumped, right in front of my eyes, and I could not do anything to stop him. Even Camila, walking away from me when I need her most.

I come from nowhere, and towards nowhere I go.

With force I run around the studio thrashing every object that gets in my way. I drag chairs and tables and pile them high in the middle of the studio. I kick and stomp over the white canvases, the paint tubes, and the easels. I go into the bedroom and turn over drawers and ransack the closets and pile all the excrements of my life into one celebratory mound sitting in the center of the studio. And on top of the mound, I position the only remaining painting, The Madonna, facing the northern window where the light is sure to shine on it.

On the floor I find the book without a title. The one I never dared to read. I grab it and consider throwing it together with the other disposable items of my life. But what is this book about? I know how it begins, but not how it ends. My right hand places the book in my pocket while my mind focuses on the task ahead.

I empty three liters of turpentine over the mortuary pyre.

I light a match.

I hear the ovation.

The combustion of my life.

I?

I contemplate the fire.

From afar, I contemplate how the harrowing red eats at the roof, the beams, my life as a painter, as a desperate seeker of nothingness. The fire helps us to forget, it uses our own substance to create light and ashes.

Consumption.

But not everything burns. My past is not flammable, nor is my desire for Camila's gentle touch, or the sense that my body belongs to the sea.

I can only eradicate one element of myself at a time. I wonder if peeling off layers will render a purer version of what I am supposed to be. Not Teaston. No. I can stop painting, I can refuse food, and I can even ignore my name, as I have already done. I can swim under the vast body of mine and resurface to breathe and look at the moon. I can do all of that, but at the end, the essence of who I am eludes me.

My death has to correspond. An unfitting death, like shoes too small or too large, is unsightly. How can I fit my death if I do not even know my name? I want death, but it must be mine.

I contemplate the fire.

The Madonna burns, with the cherubs, and the man/child on her bosom, me on her bosom, the world beneath her like the sea beneath myself.

She burns.

The fine features of a face painted centuries ago, then again by my right hand, or Phillipy's hand. In spite of her absence, hers remains the only face.

She burns.

How could you?

And how could

how could

could

you could

because that is what you did

you could and I cannot.

Can I?

The fire burning now.

You can be what you were not.

Burn, burn

no

I cannot.

Burn I say,

not all of you but the rejecting one.

Remember the drawings?

Burn I say.

The ovation reaches my ears but your words do not.

Are your words there?

Last night the moon seemed to say something. Was it the moon? And now nothing but the crackling noises of the spiteful fire.

I hear the ovation.

I hear her cry rising like a smoke spiral.

I turn to the studio, to the desecration of my life.

I am coming for you.

I run back and get as close to the fire as I can.

"Teaston."

"I'm coming for you."

As I approach the tongues of fire the heat makes the water in me boil. She is inside the mass of burning fuel. I hear her. I run around the perimeter of the studio dodging ashes. The wind blows from the south, salty, bringing the entire sea with it. And the flames rejoice at the occasion, growing tall, hungry, feasting on my life and my decrepit memories, destroying the last vestiges of my emptiness.

"Teaston, Teaston."

I try to move into the ball of fire. The hot air makes its way into my lungs and I feel the death of oxygen. My lungs draw an air that burns them. I cough and spit while my throat contracts. I step out of the fire. A smell of burnt hair poisons my stomach. A projectile vomit leaves me.

"Teaston."

"I hear you."

I look at my collapsing world as it is consumed, eaten, transformed. There is nothing to throw into the fire to stop its fury. Without a self, there is no water. The consumption rages ahead. The voices must be burning for I do not hear them now. They must be choking on the flames. I turn to the south and walk away from the flames.

I contemplate the cliff.

And as the structure of my studio collapses, I begin to bow under the pressure of a torrent of thoughts. I see how solid matter fails, consumed; I see how logic perils, raped by intruders

A face, corpses

gallop over water breaking

a rib

sink, I sink

my hand into, I cannot listen to

see how she walks with her face, not a prostitute, no

walks away with her face

all the faces the face, even before

death, as little as, I can, one part dies

my own

I do not own it, my death, no

not Teaston, even when

whiteness faints away, come in

words, words, maybe my own

grab them, grab on to the words when

to the cliff.

Tonight I am going to the edge of the cliff.

The approach is familiar, even soothing. So many times, so many opportunities to reach further, so many deaths. I see the edge and the luminous space beyond, the sea below, and my skin reflecting the moon rays. At the edge of the cliff the world is behind me, before me nothing but emptiness. The cliff awaits me. Or, is it me who has been waiting for the cliff all along? I crawl from the burning desecration of my life into the question at the very edge.

But I sense a serene light burrowing inside my brain.

The rocks are here, then the grass, soft and promising as ever

ever, will

I?

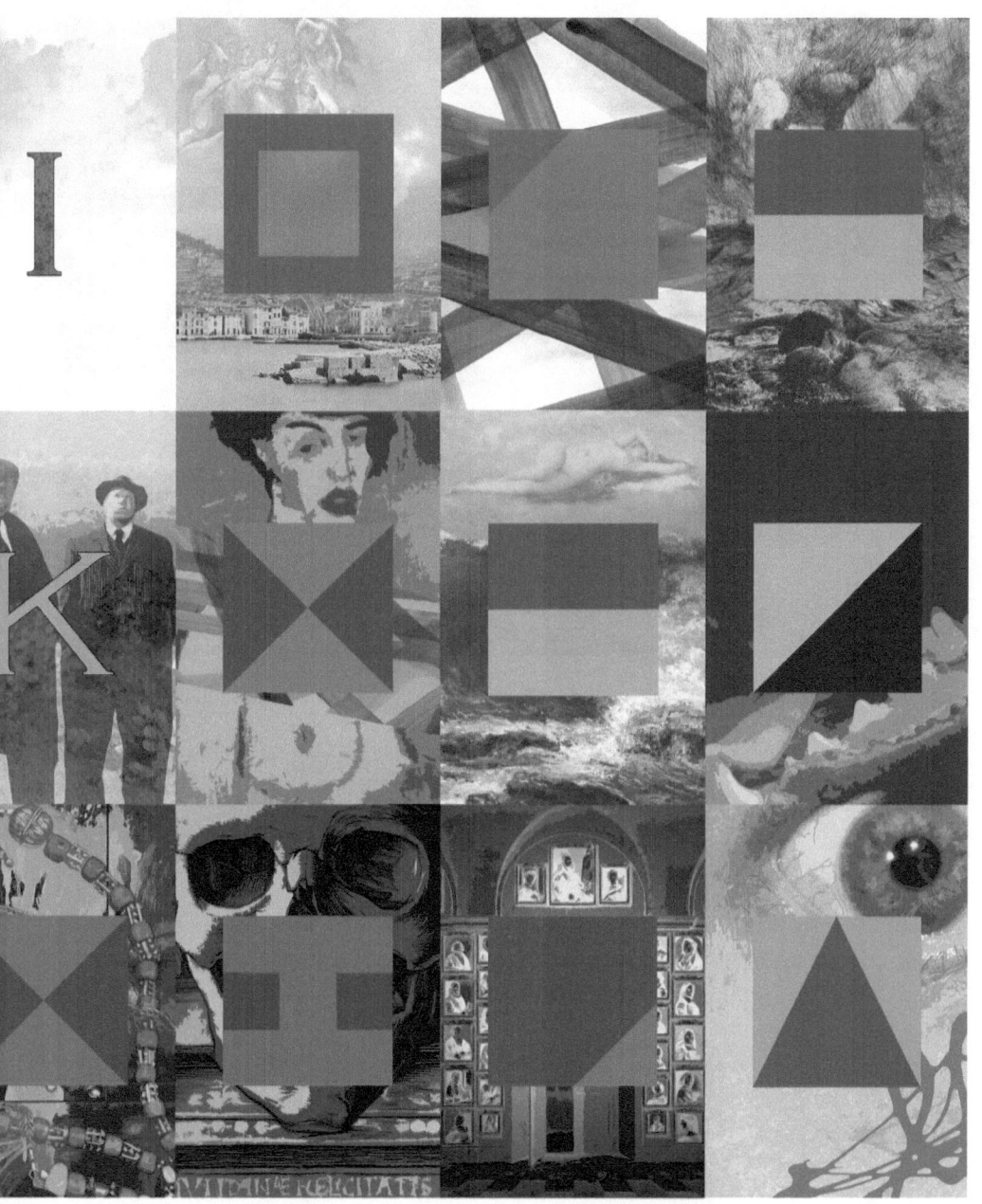

A C D E

F G H I

L M N O

S T U W

X Y (HMCB)™

HIGH MODERNIST COLOR BARCODE

About the Author

Jorge Armenteros is a practicing psychiatrist and graduate from Harvard University. In addition to his medical training, he completed an MA in Spanish and Latin American Literature from New York University, and MFA in Creative Writing from Lesley University. Born in Cuba, Armenteros now divides his time between Florida, Georgia, and the south of France.

About the Artist

Liselott Johnsson is an international artist and architect of Swedish background, who has designed architectural projects and created numerous art installations in public architectural spaces and traditional art galleries in the United States, France, British Virgin Islands and Sweden. She holds a Master of Architecture and a Master of Fine Arts in Visual Arts and is the Director of Mary S. Byrd Gallery of Art at Georgia Regents University, Augusta, GA. Her projects are featured in a variety of publications and she shares her life and creative work between Europe and the United States.

Artworks

01_cliff_I
2014, acrylic and digital painting on altered digital photo

02_woman_N_ homagetoelgreco
2014, acrylic and digital painting on altered digital photo fragment of *Annunciation*, 1590-1603, by Doménikos Theotokópoulos (El Greco)

03_bandol_T
2014, acrylic and digital painting on altered digital photo

04_faces_O _homagetoelgreco
2014, acrylic and digital painting on altered digital photo fragments of *Laocoön*, 1610-1614, *Saint Martin and the Beggar*, 1597-1599, and *Madonna and Child with Saint Martina and Saint Agnes*, 1597-1599, by Doménikos Theotokópoulos (El Greco)

05_cloud&I
2014, digital painting on altered digital photo

06_streets_T_homagetoelgreco
2014, acrylic and digital painting on vintage photo of the port of Cassis, altered digital photo fragment of *View and Plan of Toledo*, 1610-1614, by Doménikos Theotokópoulos (El Greco)
07_drip_H
2014, acrylic and digital painting

08_blacksea_E_homagetokingsley
2014, acrylic and digital painting on altered digital photo of *At Sea*, 1883, by Elbridge Kingsley

09_followme&t
2014, acrylic and digital painting, altered digital photo

10_camila&h_homagetomuybridge
2014, digital painting on digital photo collage of *Woman Walking Downstairs*, 1887, by Eadweard Muybridge

11_majesty&i_homagetotoulouselautrec
2014, digital painting on altered digital photo of work by Henri de Toulouse-Lautrec, title unknown

12_seagull&n
2014, acrylic and digital painting, altered digital photo

13_twomen&k
2014, acrylic and digital painting on digital photo collage

14_majestybreasts_S_homagetomodigliani
2014, acrylic and digital painting on altered digital photo fragment of
Female Nude with Hat, 1908, by Amedeo Modigliani

15_seaofherskin_E_homagetocourbetandcabanel
2014, acrylic and digital painting, altered digital photo fragment of
Waves, 1870, by Gustave Courbet and *The Birth of Venus*, 1863, by Alexandre Cabanel

16_wolfsmouth_A
2014, acrylic and digital painting on altered digital photo

17_sea&I_homagetokingsley
2014, acrylic and digital painting on altered digital photo of *At Sea*, 1883,
by Elbridge Kingsley

18_maman_I_homagetoelgreco
2014, acrylic and digital painting on altered digital photo fragment
of *Madonna and Child with Saint Martina and Saint Agnes*, 1597-1599, by
Doménikos Theotokópoulos (El Greco)

19_covering&A
2014, acrylic and digital painting on altered digital photo

20_bluishscars&M
2014, acrylic and digital painting on altered digital photo

21_necklace_S
2014, acrylic and digital painting on digital photo collage

22_redmind_W_homagetowechtlin
2014, acrylic and digital painting on altered digital photo of *Skull*, 1520,
by Hans Wechtlin

23_gallery_I
2014, acrylic and digital painting on altered digital photo

24_eye_M
2014, acrylic and digital painting on altered digital photo

25_ITHINKIAM_INTOTHESEAISWIM
2014, digital collage

26_ High Modernist Color Bar Code
2012-14, digital collage